Tod Benjamin's first novel was published in 2017 at the age of 81, after a long and varied life of three careers. Firstly, a five year management course led to five years as a department store manager. That was followed by twenty-five years in the chemical industry, a career that took him all over the world.

Retirement to Bournemouth to play golf and to write created the opportunity for his third career. He began to write seriously. Now, unable to play golf, he devotes most of his time to writing. With an amount of poetry, some short stories and three novels completed, *Charles and Charlie,* his second novel, is the first of The Stoker Trilogy. Book two, *The Tallyman*, continues this saga of the first half of the twentieth century through the 1930s, and the third volume, *The Soldier*, completes the story through World War 2 to 1950.

Tod Benjamin

Charles and Charlie

Book One of the
Stoker Trilogy

Austin Macauley Publishers™
London • Cambridge • New York • Sharjah

Copyright © Tod Benjamin (2020)

The right of Tod Benjamin to be identified as author of this work has been asserted by him in accordance with section 77 and 78 of the Copyright, Designs and Patents Act 1988.

All rights reserved. No part of this publication may be reproduced, stored in a retrieval system, or transmitted in any form or by any means, electronic, mechanical, photocopying, recording, or otherwise, without the prior permission of the publishers.

Any person who commits any unauthorised act in relation to this publication may be liable to criminal prosecution and civil claims for damages.

Austin Macauley is committed to publishing works of quality and integrity. In that spirit, we are proud to offer this book to our readers; however, the story, the experiences, and the words are the author's alone.

This is a work of fiction. Names, characters, businesses, places, events, locales, and incidents are either the products of the author's imagination or used in a fictitious manner. Any resemblance to actual persons, living or dead, or actual events is purely coincidental.

A CIP catalogue record for this title is available from the British Library.

ISBN 9781528980364 (Paperback)
ISBN 9781528980371 (ePub e-book)

www.austinmacauley.com

First Published (2020)
Austin Macauley Publishers Ltd
25 Canada Square
Canary Wharf
London
E14 5LQ

My sincere thanks go to all those who helped me in my efforts to establish historical facts honestly and chronologically while researching for this work. In particular, I must mention the staff at London Metropolitan University: Peter Fisher, Louise Slater and Lucy Bradley; and also Willie Watkins of the Clove Club; and not forgetting the staff of London Metropolitan Archive and the Islington Museum.

Very special thanks, though, are due to three dear friends whose knowledge of their subjects was extraordinarily valuable: Wendy Hallowell, on the complications of childbirth; Sandra Cook, on Catholicism; and my cousin Bernie Brandon on pharmacy.

Prologue
May 1926

The strong, sweet smell of leather still permeated the semi-basement that held the cobbler's workshop and, behind it, the kitchen of the flat the boy had been born in fifteen years earlier.

As he stood by the opened door at the top of the stairs leading down from the upper ground floor, the teenager felt the familiar strong odour rise and swamp over him. He had spent many hours down those stairs, watching the shoemaker create shining footwear from old, broken, worn and often dirty boots brought in by neighbours and local factory workers. Eagerly had he learned the skills of the trade from the tall man of few words who had been his gruff but kind mentor.

Today, though, the odour was sour. There was no sound of cobbling. There was stillness.

He closed the door gently so as not to disturb the silence and walked slowly into the darkened front room. His mother sat upright on the big sofa, in black from top to toe, weeping silently. He sat down beside her and placed his arm around her shoulders. For a few moments she remained rigid, but then she sagged against him, surprising him, the silent weeping becoming heavy sobs. No words passed between them. None were necessary. For him, none were possible.

The future, until now as certain as each day, was suddenly an unknown. Life had always been straightforward. He cycled to school each day; he did his homework, played sports, read books and horsed about with his pals. He ate the food that was put before him, and he slept in his own room. He completed, as well as he could, whatever household chores were demanded of him; he went to scouts every Thursday and attended Mass each

Sunday. He enjoyed the occasional family days out on weekends or during school holidays.

And, in between, he spent many, many hours downstairs with the quiet cobbler.

Some time passed before the sobbing subsided. Yet more time elapsed before Millie Stoker gathered herself together and spoke. When she did, to her son's surprise, she had instantly recovered her normal poise and firm tone:

"It's only us, now, Charlie, it's all up to us. He's gone, and he won't be back."

She paused just long enough for the words to be absorbed.

"We'll get someone to take over the workshop, and I'll get myself a bookkeeping job. You are to finish your schooling. I don't want to hear any nonsense about you doing the cobbling. You are to finish your exams and go to college. It's what your father and I struggled for, and it's what is going to happen. This tragedy will not ruin your chance in life. Now, I want you to go and do your homework."

His mother was not a big woman in any physical sense, but she was possessed of great inner strength, she had an aura. His father had been tall and broad-shouldered, a gentle giant, but it had always been she who was unquestionably in charge of the household. Charlie stood up, already five feet ten inches tall, all arms and legs, and graced with the blond hair and winning smile of his recently departed father. He stared at the woman in black for a moment, contemplating argument, but the set of her face was enough to discourage him.

"Okay, Mother." With his hands clenched fiercely at his sides, he bit back the "but I—."

Somehow, today, a gush of words was not available to him. He turned and walked into his own room. The atmosphere throughout the house was as dark as the front room curtains. He sat on the edge of his bed, eyes closed, long arms hanging between his legs, his hands linked by their touching fingertips.

The events of the past couple of days had changed life for ever. No more could he build on the dream. His grand idea of a great shoe-making business was dead. But, he asked himself, *had it ever really been alive*? He had never received any real encouragement from his parents. His mother had always said he was to go to college, but she never said what he would do afterwards, did she? Did she expect him to be a bookkeeper like Granddad Ockie? Or a bank manager? She'd done all that stuff, but it was dull stuff. He wasn't interested in those jobs, nor even being an engineer like his father, stuck in a printing works. But he did love polishing up the leather shoes and chatting with the customers in the cobbler's shop downstairs. He would have to have a serious talk with her soon. After all, he was coming up to sixteen now, not a boy anymore…nearly six feet tall, a grown man. But he had not had the courage to say that in the front room, had he?

Chapter One
The First Ten Years

Millie Stoker came from Shoreditch, just a mile down the road from the house on Amhurst Road. She had been born Mildred Cowper into a devout Catholic family, the second child of Horace Cowper, a dour and diligent clerk/bookkeeper at the local auctioneers and valuers, and his Irish wife, Doris, a seamstress. Brought up to observe the virtues of orderliness in all things and carefulness in financial matters, Milly had upheld those values throughout the years of her marriage.

In the last year or two, she had become resigned to her life. In fact, if she were honest with herself, she had become content with her life; she had felt secure. Charles Stoker had been her ideal husband. He had swept her off her feet when they first met eighteen years earlier, with his big frame, his blond hair, and that lady-killing smile. The son of a marine engineer from Liverpool, he had been raised from the age of eight in Islington. He had served a five-year apprenticeship in a printer's tool room to become a qualified engineer and toolmaker whilst also studying in the evenings at Finsbury Technical Institute to gain a degree from London University. With his acquired knowledge of photography and the printing industry, he had had a promising future in the old Battersby printing works in Clerkenwell, owned by the wealthy Collick family.

She had been an intelligent, smartly dressed, nineteen-year-old, who worked in a nearby bank. He had always maintained that he had first been attracted to her by the sight of her neatly turned ankle, espied through the window of the tool room as she dismounted from the tram one morning. He had boldly asked her to accompany him to the printworks' annual ball, where he had whirled her round the ballroom floor with grace, charm and sparkling eyes.

They had been married within nine months. At first, a small flat in Hoxton had met their needs but when she became pregnant, in the spring of 1910, she gave up her job at the bank, and Charles found them a larger home in the much smarter Amhurst Road. There, they were able to afford the considerably reduced rent of the bottom two floors of a four-storey house by agreeing to act as managing agents for the two flats above. The property was owned by the Collick family, Charles's employer.

With their own family addition imminent, they had prepared the small room next to their bedroom with great care, and when the baby was born their heaven was complete. Millie had taken one look at her new baby son and pronounced: "He's his father born again, he's a little Charlie." Her husband could only beam with pride.

Life progressed happily over the next few years. Charles thoroughly enjoyed his work and was promoted to works manager in 1911. Little Charlie was a constant source of wonder and joy to his parents, and Millie began to think of trying for a second child. They were untouched by the rumblings of strife in Europe or by the Irish troubles nearer home.

The only sadness to cloud their blue skies came with the death of Millie's father. The quiet bookkeeper, Granddad Ockie to the two-year-old, had doted upon his grandson and had visited them regularly. He contracted tuberculosis early in 1913 and died a year later, in February 1914.

Later that year, however, came an event, the consequences of which were to rock the very foundations of their little heaven. On 28th June, the Archduke Franz Ferdinand, heir to the Austro-Hungarian throne, was assassinated—with a single bullet from a Browning pistol. The complicated series of treaties and alliances established between various European nations caused a chain reaction from this tragic deed that led to Great Britain's declaration of war against Germany on 4th August.

Within a month, Charles had been encouraged by the owner of the print works, the retired Major General Sir Arthur Collick, to accept a commission as a lieutenant in the newly created photographic section of the Royal Flying Corps. He was to become a technical instructor; his expertise in the production and use of printing and photographic equipment was considered to be invaluable.

The initial wave of optimism flowing throughout the country in the late summer of 1914 suggested the war would be a brief affair. It would all be over by Christmas. Nevertheless, Millie feared the prospect. She knew her husband would accept wholeheartedly the call to serve his country, and she put on a brave face in support of his decision.

It was of comfort that her widowed mother now began to spend much of her time with her and little Charlie, the latter already a bouncy, blond, three-year-old bundle of energy. They found things to do and to laugh at that distracted her from thoughts of the ghastly war; and of her husband fiddling with photographic equipment in flying machines. Thank the Lord he was only at Farnborough and not over there. But, anyway, it would all be over soon, wouldn't it?

* * *

Charles managed to obtain leave and to get home in time for Charlie's fourth birthday. Millie marvelled at how impressive her husband looked in his new lieutenant's uniform, over six feet tall, broad shouldered, and with that smile, capable of melting icebergs. She was sure he was a wonderful instructor. He held her tightly and whispered words of love. They went to Regent's Park Zoo and showed Charlie the lions and the elephants and the chattering monkeys, much to the delight of the four-year-old. They ate ice creams and had lunch in a restaurant. They all walked to the Church of our Lady of Good Counsel on Sunday morning and received a blessing from Father Peter. All in all, they had a wonderful family weekend. But it had to end, of course, and it ended with Charles explaining to Millie that he was to undertake a pilot's training course on his return to camp.

A couple of months later, at the end of January, Charles, now Captain Stoker, managed another short weekend at home. This time he informed his wife that his squadron was going over to France within a few days. Millie remained typically silent. Charles would do what he felt to be his duty, no matter what. All he needed from her was understanding, love and support, and these she gave wholeheartedly. Only after he had left, when little Charlie was asleep and she was in the privacy of her bedroom, did she allow her frustration and resentment to show, and her tears to flow.

Clear thinking woman that she was, Millie managed to get her old job back at the bank, and she arranged for her mother to spend time with Charlie when she was at work. Charles was not to return home again for more than two years; and for much of that time Millie heard almost nothing. Newspaper reports from the Western Front told little of the stalemate that pertained across Northern France and Belgium. Reporting was fiercely censored.

There was an ongoing, but irregular, flow of mail from St. Omer in France, where Charles was attached to No.16 Squadron; but Captain Stoker's picture of events was brutally sparing. He avoided any detail of his daily life, dismissing it all as routine operations and teaching the new boys. But every letter asked about their wellbeing. How was young Charlie? Were they all well? How were they managing? Were they getting plenty of food and fuel?

Diligently, Millie replied to all his questions. While she was not one to waste words in polite conversation, her letters were as detailed as possible, filled with optimism and as much news and local gossip as she could recall; and always including the blessing received from Father Peter each Sunday morning.

In 1915, Millie concluded a significant piece of business for them. This was a negotiation with their landlords, the Collick Estate, initiated by Charles before he left Farnborough through his friend, the Hon. Stephen Collick, the Major General's nephew, to purchase the house in Amhurst Road. Millie obtained a mortgage through the good offices of her boss, the bank manager, and Charles's signatures were obtained with the assistance of the army's legal department. The income from the upper flats would offset to a considerable extent the cost of the mortgage, so that the strain on their monthly budget would be manageable.

Sometimes it was necessary for Millie to convey bad news to her husband, the worst of it being the loss, in September 1915, of her elder brother William, at Loos. Millie had never been particularly close to William, three years her elder, but her mother had now lost both the men in her life within two years and was in such a state of distress that Millie insisted she move, for the time being, into the large, under-used, downstairs front room.

However, after a week or so, Mrs Cowper, recovering somewhat, felt obliged to spend more of her time at Bethnal Green, at the home of William's widow, Dorothy. Her daughter-in-law lived with her two young children in the lower half of a house in Canrobert Street, and was in desperate need of support. Mrs Cowper continued to visit her daughter at Amhurst Road regularly, calling at least twice per week, and Florrie Brown, the daily help, willingly filled in the gaps.

The mail from France, at no time frequent, became even more scattered through 1916, but shortly before Christmas a green envelope arrived from Major Charles Stoker containing a somewhat longer letter than had been usual for him. In it Charles made no mention of his rank, but dwelt for the first time upon how much he ached to see them, to get home, to get away from 'the horror of all this misery.' The words, those written and the ones she read between the lines, formed a far more vivid picture of his situation and state of mind than previously indicated. She felt a flood of anxiety for her husband, of pride for his patriotism, and of shame for her own moments of self-pity.

It was months later, in March 1917, that she received another letter. This she read many times, then placed it carefully, separately from all the others, in the handkerchief sachet in her chest of drawers. The letter was full of an ironic lightness that was reminiscent of the pre-war Charles:

My beloved darling Millie,

Please forgive me, for I've been very careless. I was up in the clouds, flying a routine duty circuit, when I stupidly allowed the enemy to aim their guns too close for comfort. The unfortunate result was that they blew out my engine, damn them. Now, you must understand, these B.E.2s tend to go all to pieces when that happens, and the next thing I knew I was on the ground when and where I had not intended, and in a bit of a heap. Fortunately, I landed on our side of the line. Fear not, my darling, I am fine—except for a few bruises and some damage to a few bones, and to my pride.
There is a silver lining to this, though. They are going to bring me back to Blighty to sort things out, so the good of it is I shall be able to come home soon to you and Charlie. I shall keep you informed when I know more, but at least there is an end in sight, as indeed there is now to this whole ugly war. It should, hopefully, be all over soon.
Until that moment I send my deepest love,

Yours ever,
Charles

* * *

The terrible truth of his situation only became clear when, after much delay and official prevarication, mostly at Major Stoker's own instigation, he finally returned home in late January, 1918, discharged from the service, aged thirty-four, with three medals, a small pension and an artificial leg.

But the man who returned from St Omer was not the man Millie had adored and whose homecoming she had craved. The pathetic cripple who returned from France was but a shadow of her blond engineer. His cheeks were hollowed and scarred, his eyes dull, colourless and almost hidden in their deep black recesses. The blond hair was thinned, whitened and lustreless. Only in her memories and her dreams would Millie ever again feel the heat of the larger than life blond man with the wicked smile, who held her in his arms and whirled her across a ballroom floor.

Chapter Two
Life with Charles

Heart-rending as it had been, the initial shock of the homecoming was inevitably overcome, and Millie set herself the task of restoring to her beloved Charles some enthusiasm for life. She soon came to understand that the real problem was not the loss of his leg or the adjustment to the prosthesis. This was manageable. The unremitting physical pain caused by his many internal injuries and by the crude but essential life-saving treatment he had received was a far more serious problem.

The mental anguish from the shock of his experiences, and from the realisation that his careers, both army and civilian, were finished, presented an even greater challenge. But most unbearable of all for the proud engineer was that he was castrated. He was no longer a complete man, no longer capable of making love to his wife; of giving them the second child they had planned for.

Millie's down-to-earth, common-sense approach to the ordeal facing them added to her unselfish devotion to her stricken husband gradually had its effect upon him. As spring approached, she saw small signs that the weight was beginning to ease from his shoulders. He would never again be strong and there would always be pain; he would be forever coughing and needing much rest. But, as together they watched young Charlie, now nearly seven years old, playing games and being gently teased by his grandmother, she saw in Charles's eyes, just briefly, the twinkle that told her he would win this war too. He would not be defeated.

During his convalescence at the hospital in Hammersmith, Charles had been encouraged to visit the woodwork shop and to work with the equipment there; also to study the assorted manuals and how-to books that abounded on the shelves. His articulated prosthetic leg, one of the newer models developed to cope with the ever-increasing numbers required by the casualties of war, was constructed of wood and metal, with a strong, soft leather corset, crotch strap and pelvic band. Charles had worked with all these materials throughout his life and he particularly enjoyed working with leather. Slowly, he trimmed the leather to a smooth comfort, and he carefully adjusted the fit of the false limb as his scarred hip healed.

Fortuitously, the small top floor flat became vacant at about this time, and Millie, aware of Charles's determination to be active, now arranged for his father, the retired marine engineer, to sell his own house and to come to live there. The old engineer was still an active man and well able to support himself. Charles's mother had died in 1908, and his father had been living alone for ten years in a small house in Portsmouth, his home, since leaving Islington fifteen years earlier. Now, he was pleased to be able to move back to his only family, and keen to help his son in any way possible.

Millie set her father-in-law the task of converting the downstairs family room into a workshop for his son. George Stoker quickly cleared the floor and constructed a long bench across the centre of the room, with a wide shelf beneath for storage. He set it near enough to the front bay window to get the benefit of the daylight, and also built cupboards and fixtures along the two side walls for further storage and easy accessibility of tools and equipment. On the rear wall stood a large sideboard containing all Charles's old tools, packed in wooden cases and assorted boxes. The old man carefully took them out, unwrapped them one by one, and placed them on the workbench. His son, he said, could move them where he wanted them when he was ready.

Millie continued to work at the bank through 1918. There was pressure on employers to replace women with the walking wounded returning from the war, but the manager considered Millie indispensable and protected her position.

Food was now in short supply in the country and the government had introduced rationing as a precautionary measure. Millie, however, managed to ensure there was always enough food at the Stoker home. Young Charlie was at school, and Charles gradually became more active, spending the morning hours in the new workshop, organising things and fiddling with his tools or just sitting on the cushioned seat of his high, wheel-backed oak chair by the bench, gazing vacantly across the room.

On most days, his father would join him between 9.00 and 10.00 am for a morning chat, and they would share a pot of tea and whatever bakery treat Millie had left out for them, served by Florrie. Sometimes they would manage a short stroll around the block. Most afternoons Charles slept, worn out by the morning's exercise. On at least one afternoon each week, Father Peter would visit to comfort him: sitting, sharing a small whisky or two, and often dozing alongside him.

At the end of August that year, light was shining more brightly at the end of the dark tunnel of war. Alas, for the Stoker family, while the German army had been pushed back beyond the old Hindenburg Line and the Allies were advancing on all fronts, disaster now struck from an entirely different direction. The worldwide influenza virus had bypassed the family in its first wave during spring, giving a false sense of relief. Now, the virulent second wave returned to cause havoc.

Remarkably, no one in the Amhurst Road house, not even the weakened Charles, was infected; but the pandemic took the lives of poor Dorothy Cowper and her two young children. In the space of five years, Doris Cowper, Millie's mother, had lost her husband, her son, her daughter-in-law and two of her three grandchildren.

This last hammer blow was one from which the poor woman would never recover. She descended into a state of melancholia, losing all interest in the world beyond her room in Bethnal Green. Despite all of Millie's best efforts to lift her mother's depression, there was no visible response. The heartbroken woman died in the following January, from pneumonia developed from a common cold.

Millie felt the loss of her mother deeply, but recognised that it changed her life very little. Her responsibilities were to Charles and Charlie, and her energies must be concentrated upon them; plus, of course, but to a lesser extent, on old George, Charles's father, staying upstairs in the top flat. All the people she cared about were now residents of the house in Amhurst Road.

They were, of course, better off financially than most, having Charles's army pension, the income from the flats, and a small cheque received from the Collick Estate each December since Charles's enlistment in the forces. But Millie's wages were still essential for them to pay the mortgage and maintain their standard of living; and with her mother no longer visiting two days a week, it became necessary to employ Florrie Brown for the whole week. The domestic help was not a costly expense but nevertheless placed further strain on the household budget.

Fortunately, Charles felt he was now reaching the point where he could do something about it.

* * *

Although the war ended with the armistice of 11th November 1918, the economic aftereffects of the conflict were felt as heavily by the victors as by the vanquished. Economic depression brought widespread unrest throughout the country. In 1919, there were more British than German workers involved in strikes. By 1921, unemployment in England reached over eleven percent, the highest rate since records had begun. Swingeing cuts in public spending were introduced to ward off inflation.

At the Stoker home in Amhurst Road, though, things were going comparatively well. With his father's help and contacts, Charles acquired a second-hand treadle sewing machine from a supplier in Portsmouth, a model 29K Singer, the best machine in the world for shoemaking or shoe repairing. The machine was installed behind the workbench, carefully placed so that Charles could swing easily from one surface to the other. Most of the other tools he required were already in his possession, and were now placed in strategic positions around the room.

Hackney was an established shoe manufacturing area, so the leather and other materials he might need were readily available from the hand grindery merchants in the district. It only required, early in July 1919, a small notice to be placed in the top corner of the downstairs front window and an advertisement printed in the Hackney Gazette, for business to begin to trickle in.

Charles, the war casualty and cobbler, could cope with only a very limited amount of work at first, so the small volume of customers suited him. His father came down to help out for a couple of hours each day when he became busier, and as he grew stronger and more confident the trickle became a steady flow. People, mostly neighbours or others known to them, quickly recognised the quality of his work and spread the word.

Charles found himself tied to the bench for a great part of each day from Monday to Saturday. Physically, the determined engineer coped quite well, moving around more and more easily as time passed. But the constant pain he suffered and endeavoured to hide from his customers took its inevitable toll. Never the most loquacious of people, he spoke less and less, creating the impression that he was a brooding, silent man, preoccupied solely with perfecting his shoemaking skills.

Millie, of course, never saw him thus. To her, he was still her handsome hero, the wooden leg a mere encumbrance. He would always be her one and only, her twinkle-eyed lover; his inability to physically fulfil the role was an irrelevance. That twinkle, sadly, was rarely seen during the long working week.

At weekends, his old spirit was a little more visible, albeit still subdued. He would relax with young Charlie in the workshop, teaching him how to work the leather: how to soften it, how to trim it, to buff it, to polish it. Although he never spoke of his experiences in the war, he taught his young son how to send messages in Morse code, as he had done a few years earlier in the Royal Flying Corps. He built a crystal set, with which they listened to some of the early radio transmissions from Marconi's Station 2MT at Writtle. Much of the time, though, he would just sit and watch his son's activity and listen to the nine-year-old chatter, the barest of smiles playing across his scarred features.

The steadily increasing income from the shoe repairing had eased their financial problems to such an extent that by the end of 1920 Millie gave up her full-time position at the bank. Having worked there for so many years, she had become a highly skilled and experienced book-keeper. She had also established an excellent relationship with the manager, who willingly allowed her a shorter working week in order to retain some of her usefulness. From her point of view, she could now spend more time with young Charlie.

Kodak Brownie cameras had by this time made photography available to everyone at a very low cost, and Millie purchased a folding Autographic camera for £4.10s. She was thus able to record every important moment in their lives for the cost of a roll of 120 film per eight pictures.

Charlie, already ten years of age, was approaching the time when he could take the scholarship examination for the grammar school at Hackney Downs. The boy did not really need extra coaching, he loved school and learned eagerly, but Millie was not one to take chances. Everything went according to plan, and Charlie, in smart blazer and flannels, entered the first year at Hackney Downs School in September of 1921. He was a fine-looking boy, tall for his age, with a quick mind and a winning smile, inherited from his father. He soon became popular at the grammar school.

* * *

The death of George Stoker was a sudden tragedy that came as a particularly heavy blow to Charles and was the next in the stream of tragic events that bore upon the family. The old man had spent most of the last few years with his son, chatting, encouraging and assisting him in his work and his adjustment to life after France.

At sixty-seven years of age, George Charles Stoker was still very active and to all intents and purposes a fit man. He had his routine of regular daily walks and helping in the workshop for a couple of hours; but he also enjoyed reading in the privacy of his flat at the top of the house.

Late in 1922, he had been suffering from a persistent head cold with what he assumed was an associated series of headaches. When one morning he was found dead at the bottom of the stairs, the subsequent examination revealed that a brain tumour had caused a fatal haemorrhage. He was buried on 2nd December.

After this, much of the zest for life Charles had so laboriously regained seemed to leak from him. Even the hours spent with his son were now insufficient to give more than the faintest relief from his depression and constant pain. The atmosphere in the house became darker and more silent. The weekend outings the family had enjoyed became more and more occasional. Charles was coughing a great deal, his daily load sapping his energy.

It was beginning to affect his work, so Millie took charge of all the paperwork to ease the strain. Young Charlie willingly helped out in the workshop in the evenings and at weekends, whenever his school activities allowed, and with the boy's youthful energy and Millie's calm control, business continued at just about an acceptable level.

The year 1923 saw the signing of the Lausanne Treaty, the final treaty necessitated by the Great War. It signalled the end of the Ottoman Empire, the last of the four great empires to be toppled by the conflict. The Russian, German, and Austro-Hungarian regimes had already been crushed. The treaties, though, did not bring much economic relief to Europe. Unemployment in England had remained at its double-figure post-war level, and was now expected to remain so for the foreseeable future.

The poor people of Hackney and Dalston wore their shoes almost down to the seams before taking them to the cobbler, but Charles's patient skill invariably made them wearable again for a small fee. The workshop had now been open for four years and, although a large store of customer loyalty had been accumulated, the sombre figure of the shoe repairer did little to encourage many new visitors throughout 1923. As time passed, though, as had happened after Charles's return from France in 1917, Millie's calm presence and constant attention gradually had their effect.

To some degree, the wounded man yet again recovered his old persona, and there appeared just occasionally the faint twinkle in his eye that told his wife her efforts were not in vain. Young Charlie's presence in the workshop, particularly on Saturdays, always lifted the atmosphere. The twelve-year-old's enthusiasm and laughing, cheeky comments endeared him to one and all. The Stoker smile seemed to overcome all obstacles. The wolf was once more kept from the door, and quiet peace reigned for a year or two.

Throughout the years before and after his father's death, regardless of the constant pain he bore and about which he never complained, Charles rose at 6.00 am every day, went for a morning walk, opened the shop at 7.30 am and closed for lunch at 11.45 am. He would allow himself a short nap after lunch before re-opening at 1.00 pm. The afternoons, it always seemed to Millie, he found less of a strain, partly, no doubt, because of the lunchtime rest, but partly in anticipation of young Charlie's bubbling presence later on.

When Millie's boss, the bank manager, retired in the summer of 1924, his replacement had his own ideas and made Millie redundant. Fortunately, Charles, with the aid of the rental incomes, was now earning enough to maintain the household. The volume of business even justified taking on an apprentice in the mornings.

Young Charlie's assistance was consequently less essential and the boy was encouraged to devote more time to his studies and to his extra-curricular activities. He had proved to be very bright at school, and in September 1925 he began his studies for the matriculation examinations of June 1926. His parents had decided that, all being well, he would afterwards work towards a university degree.

Twenty years earlier, Charles himself had received a degree in physics and mechanical engineering from London University by attending evening classes for five years at

Finsbury Technical Institute. He had fond memories of the institute and had hoped that young Charlie would perhaps try for a similar qualification, but by studying as a full-time student. Now, however, the future of the Institute was under severe threat. It was due to be closed with all study courses being transferred to the Central College of the City and Guilds Institute in Kensington. Islington Council was fighting the closure but it looked likely that it would fail to influence the decision. Charles, although disappointed, was consoled by the thought that Charlie may instead find a good place at the university.

As an encouragement, for his fifteenth birthday, Charles and Millie bought Charlie a Raleigh bicycle with a Sturmey-Archer three-speed gear. Charlie was a keen cyclist and a keen student. He was delighted with his new bike but he didn't really care about university. What he wanted to do was to work in the now quite substantial family business. He harboured dreams of making shoes and of building a great enterprise.

Charlie accepted with teenage reluctance that his parents knew best, but that did not prevent him from expounding his grandiose schemes at length to the silent man on the high chair, rarely receiving more than a nod or an occasional half-smile in acknowledgement. When really pressed to reply, Charles would sigh and mumble something like: "Ye-es, it would be nice. We shall have to wait and see. You need your studies first."

* * *

1925 came to a close and young Charlie's matriculation exams came ever nearer in a world that was again becoming more troubled. The economic difficulties plaguing the country since the Great War had encouraged ever greater militancy in the trade union movement, fanned by strong communist influences. When, earlier in the year, the recently elected Conservative government had returned sterling to the gold standard, the resultant depression had given cause to the strongly unionised miners, together with their triple alliance comrades, the railwaymen and the transport workers, to call for a strike for better wages and shorter hours. This had been averted for nine months by the government's payment of a wages subsidy; but when the subsidy ended, in March of 1926, the mine owners did not offer to reduce hours, but contrarily drew up plans to increase them and to cut pay.

At a TUC Conference on 1st May, a national general strike was agreed. The following day, an edition of the Daily Mail, the paper with the largest circulation in the country, was prepared, attacking the miners as 'a revolutionary movement'. The workers in the newspaper's print room refused to print it. This caused havoc and all negotiations collapsed. The general strike went ahead on 3rd May 1926.

In Hackney, the Workers Council of Action huffed and puffed from the headquarters it had set up in a local boxing hall. It succeeded in organising a number of disruptive stoppages in the Conservative controlled borough. The larger places of employment were picketed: no trams could leave the depot and the local paint and furniture factories were forced to close.

A number of minor fracas occurred but strike breakers also had their successes. A notable one was achieved by three boys of the Clove Club (Ex-pupils from Charlie's school), who maintained a train service between Liverpool Street and Chingford throughout the twelve-day period of the strike.

With the main local employers shut down and the tram depot paralysed, Millie ensured that young Charlie left early for school each day. The teenager and his school friends, however, were for the most part unaffected by the strike, apart from the excitement caused by the wild gossip that ensued daily from the situation.

As for business, shoemaker Charles found that he was free to carry on his work but with very few customers. Billy Walters, his young apprentice-assistant, was keen to continue working and Charles had not the heart to lay him off, so, during the week, he left Billy in charge of the empty workshop and took advantage of the lack of trade to go out for daily strolls. He wanted to see for himself what things were like around the district.

Charles had disassociated himself from all his pre-war friendships after 1918, but by now he had become a well-respected citizen, known locally as Major Charles, the retired Royal Flying Corps pilot. He was easily recognised with his tall frame, his walking stick and his limp. His morning walks were always punctuated by a series of greetings and short chats wherever he found himself as he wandered through the streets.

On the third day of the strike, the 5th May, his chosen route took him into Kingsland Road, where he found himself unexpectedly caught up with a huge and noisy crowd. Some horse vans and a couple of motorised lorries had been declared by the strike leaders to be 'black' transport. They were being manhandled by a belligerent gang of angry strikers. There were crowds of people standing all around, some voicing encouragement to the strikers, some shouting abuse. Policemen were present in force on the south side of the obstructed area and were clearly preparing for action.

The atmosphere quite quickly became threatening. More police arrived on the north side of the crowd and Charles heard an officer cry out, "Charge the Bastards!" In a moment, the scene was transformed. Anxious to avoid being crushed by the crowd, Charles attempted to turn back but found his way blocked by charging policemen and panicking bystanders.

Truncheons waving, the police attacked from both ends of the jammed area. They launched themselves at the ragged gang with arms flailing, knocking them down, scattering them into each other and into the crowd of onlookers and passers-by. Men, women and a number of children were sent flying and trampled over by the onrushing mass of uniforms.

Everything happened far too quickly for Charles. A sudden surge of bodies threw him against a doorway, causing him to lose his balance. His head cracked against the hard stone of the supporting door frame and his walking stick flew up in the air. He tumbled headlong to the ground, ignored and trodden upon by the turbulent mass of fleeing troublemakers and panicked spectators; and completely disregarded by the single-minded, heavy-booted policemen relentlessly chasing, beating, kicking, and arresting their targets.

Order was quickly restored. Charles was recognised and medical help was summoned. He was rushed to Homerton Hospital. A police constable was sent to inform Millie of the situation, and she was escorted to her husband's bedside.

Millie arrived at the hospital to find her beloved Charles lying quite still, unconscious and very pale. She sat for many hours, waiting and praying for her beloved to awaken and to smile at her. But there came no smile. There was no awakening.

Charles Stoker died that evening without recovering consciousness.

Chapter Three
1926, The Collick Estate

Millie appeared to exist in a mental vacuum, almost as if in a coma, for days after Charles's death. Other than when dealing with her son or answering a direct question, she sat, silent on the big sofa, staring blankly ahead. Father Peter had comforted Millie Stoker through many painful experiences over the years but nothing had quite compared to this. Well aware that this could be one calamity too many, he visited daily to sit and comfort her. He held her hand, whispering his unique Irish blend of compassionate words and light, invariably one-sided, conversation.

There were times when the priest felt overwhelmed by his own doubts, his inability to comprehend the ways of the Lord. Yet never for one second had he failed in his duty of care for his flock; and Charles and Millie Stoker had always been at the heart of that flock. For eight years, Millie Stoker had striven to guide her beloved Charles back to some sort of contentment with life; and to give their beloved child a happy upbringing, even as so many family members were being taken from her one by one. Now, seeing her suffer the horrific events of the first week of May and trying to help her through the ordeal, to enable her to deal with the consequences, caused his compassion to overflow. Gently, slowly, he encouraged her to recover a sense of purpose in life; and, eventually, her remarkable strength of character began to re-assert itself.

Millie began to plan for the future. Once recovered from her traumatic reaction to *that* day, she dealt with the practical matters of financial and household affairs with her usual calm efficiency. Events evolved so that she did not feel obliged to sell the business or to take another job. Instead, she made Billy Walters the manager. He was very young, but he was capable and personable. He had quickly grown into the job, and trade was healthy.

Millie retained control of the book-keeping and purchasing, operating quietly behind the scenes. On the rare occasions when she needed guidance in their affairs, she was accorded access to advice from an unexpected but powerful source.

A service of remembrance had been held for Charles six weeks after his death, in which both his brave war effort and his local esteem were respectfully recognised. Many local dignitaries had been present, including the mayor, the police superintendent and the local union leaders, together with the majority of the small Catholic congregation.

Most notably represented was the Collick Estate, in the persons of Charles's old boss, Major General Sir Arthur Collick, now somewhat tottery in his late seventies, and his nephew, the Hon. Stephen Collick, younger son of Lord Collick, Sir Arthur's elder brother, who had died in 1922. The elder son, Roderick, had acceded to the barony, but it was Stephen, the second son, a severe looking forty-three-year-old bachelor, who had since become the driving force in the family's business enterprises.

Stephen Collick, who had facilitated their purchase of the house in Amhurst Road eleven years earlier, had been close to Charles before the war, and it was he who led Millie quietly to one side after the service. The Collick family, he said, was conscious of its responsibility toward Charles's family. Charles had been a shining light in the fast-growing printing works in 1914. He had been a man of imagination and invention, and it had been their intention, if the war had not intervened, that Sir Arthur would retire after a few years, and Charles would become the managing director of the printing company.

Sadly, war service and Charles's terrible injuries had put paid to their plans. Indeed, he himself had been abroad with the Essex Regiment in the Sinai in 1917 and had only discovered Charles's true condition on his return home after the armistice.

"Mrs Stoker," he continued earnestly, "Your husband was a hero. His daring work with our quite untested equipment in France contributed greatly to this country's cause. He was a brave and honourable man, and, I will say, a gentleman, a modest and independent gentleman. When, during his rehabilitation, we attempted to assist and to compensate him, he refused to permit it. He was adamant. His only concession was to allow the annual allowance, pittance that it is, to be continued for his lifetime. Beyond that, he said, his family was his own responsibility. He would not allow the estate to help him any further. He insisted he be left to plough his own furrow."

"Thereafter, my uncle retired, the printing works was placed under new management, and I was forced to turn my attention to our other ventures. As you are aware, I maintained contact at a distance, but I and my family have always known that we have an obligation to care for the Stoker family."

Stephen Collick paused at this point, wearing a distinctly crestfallen look. Then he resumed in the same earnest tone: "Now, sadly, the tragedy of Charles's sudden death has endangered your family's very existence, and the Collick Estate intends to ensure that certain actions are taken to protect you."

These actions, he explained, would make life a little more comfortable for them. Firstly, the Collick Estate would ensure that the annual cheque she had been accustomed to receiving would be doubled, and would be paid as long as she lived. Secondly, the outstanding mortgage on the house would be cleared so that the income from rentals would be sufficient for a comfortable living. Thirdly, he, Steven Collick, would ensure, when the time came for young Charlie to start out on a career, that there be an opportunity for him within the Collick enterprises. He would, he emphasised, consider it a privilege to employ Charles Stoker's son.

After another short pause, during which Millie continued to stand, still and silent as a statue, her face a blank mask, the sad-faced man ended with an astonishing personal commitment. He would, he said, be available at any time, then or in the future, for advice or support, should she or her son ever need it. He would consider it as more than a privilege: it would be an honour to be regarded as a family friend. It was the very least he could offer to compensate for the pain and sadness his family had unwittingly initiated twelve years earlier.

The newly-widowed Millie stood, speechless probably for the first time in her life, as the morning-suited baron's son awkwardly made to shake hands in a stiff gesture of his sincerity. After a hiatus of two or three seconds, during which the businessman became clearly ill-at-ease, she raised herself onto her toes and kissed him briefly on the cheek.

"Thank you, sir. You are a fine gentleman," she said softly.

"Please," he replied, grasping her arms with both hands and pressing them to her sides, "I beg you, call me Stephen."

Millie, with the faintest of smiles, inclined her head in acknowledgement.

* * *

Later, in the still cold comfort of her home, Millie considered what Stephen Collick had told her. The unexpected generosity of the Collicks would be of enormous benefit to her and to Charlie. It would completely relieve the financial strain on the household budget, so long as the rentals were secure and there were no unforeseen difficulties with the shoe-repair business. Not that either possibility was likely. There was a constant demand for the flats and she was able to be quite selective in choosing her tenants, most of whom stayed for at least a couple of years.

As for the repair shop, that was now a well-established business. She herself kept the books, and she included in her costing a regular charge for the use of the premises. Billy Walters was a first-class worker and an ambitious young man. He regarded his position as a career for life and fully intended to prove his worth and to develop the business further. Millie recognised his value and ensured he was well rewarded, although Billy understood that it was up to him to justify his income. His only financial involvement was in selecting materials as he needed them and ensuring that the income he generated was always enough to cover the costs. The better he performed, the more he would be rewarded, but if the cobbling became unprofitable she would close it down.

At eighteen years of age, Billy had risen well to the change in his situation. He realised that the tragedy of 5th May presented him with an opportunity he could never have anticipated. In the two years he had been apprenticed to Major Charles Stoker he had learned his trade well. He was full of admiration for Major Charles, who had taught him thoroughly and patiently, even on those days when it was clear the poor man had been in terrible pain. Not that he had ever mentioned it, but at times he would sit down heavily on that high stool and sigh, and remain absolutely silent for several minutes. Sometimes, he went nearly the whole morning without speaking at all.

But, *that* morning, he must have been feeling extra well, because all of a sudden, he had said: "I think you know it all now, Billy, so while it's quiet, I'm going to leave you in charge. I want to have a look around the area, to see whether this world of ours is remaining intact, despite the efforts of these communist agitators to control our workers, sheep that they are."

It had been a big speech for the Major, and Billy never saw him again. Now it was really down to him. Mrs Stoker had given him the chance to run the shop and he would never forget that.

* * *

Millie had met Mr Collick on one or two occasions through the years, but, apart from very early in her marriage, always briefly, on matters of business. Her impression of him had always been of a rather distant, cold type. What a transformation she had seen today! Such a sad face, such a diffident manner…

Although everything he had said was quite formally expressed, she had detected an earnestness in him, a gentleness, indeed a sadness, perhaps one caused by more than just the day's tragic occasion. Even so, he had triggered one or two disturbing thoughts.

His opening words came back to her as she sat on the big sofa in the front room. *Your husband was a hero. His daring work with our quite untested equipment in France contributed greatly to this country's cause.* What exactly had he meant? What was daring about the work had Charles undertaken? *With our untested equipment*? Charles had always said he was training men to use photographic equipment, but had sworn he was not near the front line; that is, until that last letter.

That letter…she knew it word for word. She did not need to go to her handkerchief drawer, she could see the words in her head: *Fortunately, I landed on our side of the line.* Had he been flying in enemy territory, then? What secret endeavours had endangered, no, ruined his life? And what had it to do with the Collicks?

There was something else that Stephen Collick had said, what was it? Millie cast her mind back to the scene. Ah, yes, something or other…*offer to compensate for the pain and sadness his family had unwittingly initiated twelve years earlier.* That was it. *His family had initiated…* Had Charles not been open with her? Had his enlistment been triggered by something other than patriotism? Had he been involved in some secret hanky-panky that he had not trusted her enough to confide? Were there things she been blind to all these years?

His medals…they had never really spoken about them, had they? He had said they were what everyone in the RFC received, and they had just lain in that box. He never looked at them and she had never thought to. His sickness and his care were all that she had ever concerned herself with. When people called him a hero, she assumed it was because he flew aeroplanes and because he lost a leg. How blinkered had she been all these years?

She drew a deep breath. Well, what did any of it matter now? Charles was dead. After all those years of misery and pain, he would feel pain no more, thanks be to the Lord.

She sat quietly for a few minutes, then the resentment hidden within her welled up once more and tears ran down her cheeks.

"But I do!" she screamed to the empty room.

Chapter Four
1928 – The Northern

Young Charlie had often cycled past the imposing building in Holloway Road that housed beneath its white clock tower the Northern Polytechnic Institute. Recently, he had entered its front doors on a few occasions for interviews, but on this pleasant September day in 1928 he entered for the first time as a student, to commence a three-year course for a Bachelor of Science degree in Physics and Engineering from London University.

The headmaster of Hackney Downs School, Mr W Jenkyn-Thomas, had thought—no, he had expected—his senior prefect to apply to an Oxford college. As one of the school's star pupils, with top grade results at matriculation and again at scholarship level, acceptance was assured, he had insisted. Millie Stoker, though, was adamant. Her husband had studied at Finsbury Technical Institute and had wanted his son to follow him there. On the closure of that facility in 1926, the very year of her husband's death, the Institute had been absorbed into the Northern Polytechnic, so that was where Charlie was to go. As far as she was concerned, the matter was settled. Mr Jenkyn-Thomas raised his hands in frustration but conceded the argument.

The decision meant that Charlie could cycle to the college each day and home again each evening. Thus, he would still be close to his mother, his only living relative. As she had so succinctly expressed in the darkened front room on the day of the burial: *"It's only us, now, Charlie. He's gone, and he won't be back."*

Millie had always been, in Charlie's eyes, a rather austere figure, cool, capable, but not easily approachable. However, her manner had softened considerably after *that day*—the only term his mother used when referring to the day of his father's death—and the relationship between mother and son had become somewhat easier over the next couple of years.

Physically, Charlie was very much his father's son. Already over six feet tall, if as yet with an unfilled frame, he had inherited the smile that had so won his mother's heart twenty years earlier. Watching his father day after day, he had learned that a smile and an interested gaze usually encouraged others to open up, to say things.

In the two sixth form years since *that* day, the rangy prefect had carefully cultivated what had been a natural trait in his father, and he found himself to be in high demand by the various school clubs and common room cliques. He had joined the cycling club and loved the long rides. No longer the chatterbox of his childhood, he was mostly content to let others do the talking. It was enough for him to be present among them with his occasional surprising sharp wit, and the ever-present twinkle in his eye, beneath a mop of blond hair.

At home, life was generally quiet yet strangely comfortable. Downstairs in the workshop Billy would always be busy, with or without customers, but Charlie visited him only occasionally. His mother would be in the kitchen or in her large bedroom, where she attended to the bookwork. He spent most of his time in his own room, studying or reading.

At his pre-assessment interview with the Principal and the Head of the Department two weeks earlier, he had learned that his excellent matriculation and sixth form university scholarship results at Hackney Downs exempted him from the first-year pure mathematics classes and from about half of the first-year physics course. This meant that he would have a considerable number of free periods for the first year.

Now, entering the spacious reception hall on this Wednesday morning, his first day as a college student, Charlie was confronted by an array of notice boards full of timetables for all the courses available for the academic year. The place was a hive of activity as the six or seven hundred day students rushed to their classes or, if first-timers, brushed against each other as they hustled to find their bearings, to gather their relevant information from the notices, and to record their presence to the clerks at the table placed in front of the office.

Charlie's course would include some chemical engineering, instrument making and some metal work, as well as applied mathematics. He was excited to be beginning this, his father's course, although he was not at all sure of its relevance to his own ideas for the future. He had always enjoyed being in the shoemaker's workshop, but he was not keen to spend his working life behind that big bench or in some factory tool room.

Creating things with his hands was fun, but what had excited him, ever since he had been allowed to share the experience, had been chatting to all the people who came through the door. It was exciting to learn about their families and how they managed from day to day; to hear about their lives – lives lived, to his young ears, in seemingly different worlds from the one he knew in the tall house with its basement workshop and its walled kitchen garden. Their stories, their troubles and their pleasures were the things that really fired Charlie's imagination.

He was wearing his father's best suit, a dark blue double-breasted woollen worsted with fine white pinstripes running through. Although he had reached his father's height, he was still quite slim, and his mother had spent many hours altering seams and steam-pressing the suit to make it a perfect fit for this auspicious day. The accomplished book-keeper was also an accomplished seamstress, a skill learned from her mother as a young girl. Her unemotional competence made Charlie doubly proud to honour his father's memory in this way.

As he looked around, though, he felt a little overdressed. The majority of students seemed to be about his age, but nearly all were in rough working clothes: heavy trousers and jackets or thick jumpers; a number of them in dark blue boiler suits. Their chatter was principally about the Olympic Games, held a few weeks earlier in Amsterdam, or about Arsenal's prospects in the football season just beginning. Both subjects were of little interest to Charlie, although he had read reports in the *Daily Mail*.

Many of the students were signing in for tradesman classes; some for mathematics and other matriculation studies, but almost none for the degree courses. Indeed, there were a mere twenty-four names on the notice board for the physics department, and similarly small numbers for the chemistry, geology and botany courses.

Charlie took a notebook from his satchel and copied the details of his timetable into it, then joined the registration queue. At the office, he collected his text books and an assortment of course papers, including a typed sheet containing all the timetable information he had so studiously copied from the notice board minutes earlier. He sorted it all into the copious satchel, then paid three shillings for the key to a locker in which to keep his lunch box and personal belongings during the year.

The final duty of the morning, at 10.30 am, was to take a seat in the Great Hall, where, for thirty minutes or more, the principal, Dr R. S. Clay, addressed the year's new students and, as Charlie freely interpreted to his mother that evening, "filled us all with enthusiasm and told us where the lavatories were."

On this first day of term, studies were to begin after lunch and his classes were to be physics from 1.30 to 3.00 pm, then applied mathematics until 4.30 pm. This left him with plenty of time to wander around and familiarise himself with the college layout. He headed for the lockers to deposit his satchel and books, then, with a physics book under his arm, he strolled along the corridor towards the rear of the building and the refreshment area.

Unlike standard college refectories, the huge rectangular space was filled with twelve heavy oak tables. Each table could seat up to about ten students on wooden chairs. The principal had mentioned in his introductory address that senior students could order luncheon for nine pence per day, but Charlie intended to bring his own lunch and to eat outside whenever the weather permitted. He entered the room. There were a few students sitting in clusters. Since it was only a little after eleven o'clock, the place was not yet busy, morning sessions for existing students not finishing until noon or half-past. He spent three pence on a pot of tea and a bath bun, and settled at the end of an unoccupied table halfway down the room. He poured some tea, munched a large chunk of bath bun and began to study the physics text book.

* * *

"Let's sit here and have a cigarette, Daphne, there's a nice bit of space."

Charlie glanced up from his book at the sound of a voice close by. The words came from a young lady of about his own age standing at the other end of his table on the opposite side. She was quite petite, and she struggled to drag a large briefcase onto the chair next to her before sitting herself down. Charlie returned his attention to physics, but his subconscious brain registered that this was a girl well worth a second look. He raised his head again, at the precise moment that she glanced along the table. Their eyes met briefly. She blushed, quickly lowered her head and turned to face her friend Daphne, her voice dropping to a whisper.

Charlie continued to look. The girl was attractive and very smartly dressed. She wore a soft green, finely knitted suit with a wide-pleated skirt and a round-necked top with three wide V-shaped white stripes that led the eye down to the wide belt at the outfit's dropped waist. Her short, light brown hair was mostly hidden under a dark green cloche hat, just a ringlet visible above her left eye. Charlie, impressed, but conscious that he too looked impressive in his father's suit, smiled to himself and returned his attention to tea and physics.

Having enjoyed his leisurely refreshment, he then continued on his familiarisation journey, exchanging a second glance with Daphne's friend as he stood up to leave. His wide grin was met with a blush and a brief smile from her grey-green eyes before she again turned quickly away.

A notice on the wall outside the refreshment area directed him along a short corridor and down some stairs to the empty gymnasium. It was larger than the one at Hackney Downs, but

Charlie was not excited by the sight. Although tall and with an athletic frame, he was no longer an enthusiastic gymnast. In truth, he had lost his early eagerness for most school sports. He loved riding his bike and quite enjoyed swimming but had lost all interest in field sports.

He re-mounted the stairs, walked past the kitchens and the dressmaking room, and found himself passing through the building department. A building laboratory and a row of busily occupied classrooms led to double doors, beyond which were separate buildings housing welding, plumbing and carpentry workshops and a forge. Next to the forge, at the rear of the cycle shed, was a path that led him back to the front of the college.

Now with a clear picture of the layout, Charlie re-entered by the front door, collected his packed lunch from his locker and went out again. With the physics book and his lunch box under his arm he walked the few hundred yards down Holloway Road to the St Mary Magdalene Gardens, one of Highbury's pretty green spaces. Once a burial ground, it was now a public park, and he had often sat under the majestic plane trees with a couple of cycling friends when in the sixth form at Hackney Downs. On this occasion, though, he sat on a bench seat by one of the ornamental rose gardens.

"Ha-allo! It's young Charlie, Major Stoker's son, surely?"

Charlie turned from studying his lunch box to see the smiling, weather-beaten features of an elderly gardener, pushing a wheelbarrow full of gardening equipment,

"I'm sorry, I don't... Oh, yes I do! It's Mr Biskin, isn't it? How are you, I haven't seen you for years! I didn't know you worked over here."

Charlie stood up to shake the gardener's hand. Arthur Biskin had been one of the shoe repairer's very first customers, a chatty soul who lived with his wife and family just around the corner from the cobbler in Coronation Avenue. He regularly brought the family footwear into the shop for new heels or soles, but, of course, since *that* day Charlie had not been in the workshop, except for fleeting visits to see Billy.

"Oh, yes, indeed, I work for the council," the gardener replied with pride. "I've worked here for years, looking after these gardens, yes, I have. I've been very fortunate, yes, to be sure. But you, you've grown so tall! You're as tall as your late father, may he rest in peace."

He broke off as if suddenly recalling the event, then shook his head. "He was a fine man, wasn't he? An honourable man. He flew in the war, of course."

He shook his head again and tutted.

"What a terrible business that was, and he such a respected personage."

His brow furrowed and he shook his head again, "And all because of that benighted strike. They called it the 'General Strike' and claimed they were fighting for the workers, but no-one I knew wanted to strike, let alone cause havoc in the streets."

He paused again and scratched his head. "But then, sir, I always had a safe job and many others did not, that's a fact. I suppose one has to see their side of it too, don't you think?"

Charlie, bemused, just gazed at the gardener, unable to muster words for a reply. Mr Biskin, embarrassed, changed the subject,

"I see you're taking your lunch in the lovely September sun today, eh?"

"Yeah, er, yes, it is a fine day. I've just started at the Polytechnic today and I had an hour to spare before my first lesson, so I was reading my physics book. But it's nice to see you again, Mr Biskin."

"And you, young sir, and you. Do give my best regards to your mother. I expect we shall be round there quite soon to give more work to young Billy."

He picked up his wheelbarrow and went on his way. Charlie tried to return to his physics book but Mr Biskin's words had struck a strange chord in his mind. For the first time since *that* day, he found himself thinking about the tragedy in a different light. Not once had he ever thought of the death of his father as other than a disaster caused by a riot of hooligans. Now, suddenly, he was glimpsing what the incident may have meant to others. When Mr Biskin said '*one has to see their side of it too',* did he mean his father's death was sad but was just a part of the price to be paid because the workers had to fight for jobs? Was he saying having a job was more important than his dad's life? That's not right, surely. If you want to work, you can always get another job, but you can't get another life.

Charlie had been brought up to believe that life was sacred. Father Peter talked, Sunday after Sunday, about God caring for us and us caring for each other. His mother had cared for and nursed his father for years and years. People did not cry for two years over a lost job, like his mother had cried every night for his father. She thought he didn't know, but he had heard her through the door of her room time and again. You're wrong, Mr Biskin, there isn't another side to it.

* * *

Science classrooms, laboratories and lecture rooms were on the first and second floors, the physics section being on the upper level. There were two lecture rooms and three laboratories. Charlie strode up the first flight of stairs and screamed to a halt halfway up the second flight behind the two girls from the refreshment room, the pretty one having stopped to put down her heavy briefcase.

"Let me carry that up," said Charlie, whisking the briefcase from the stair tread with a twinkling smile at the girl in green. He brushed past both ladies to hoist it up to the landing. The surprised recipient of his attention hurried up the remaining stairs behind him, admonishing him:

"That's very kind of you, but I could manage perfectly well myself, thank you." The words came in an embarrassed rush as the girl, blushing, reached up to take back the briefcase that Charlie, towering above her, was holding high in the air. The tall Charlie laughed and lifted the case away from her. "Which room are you heading for?"

"Oh, Physics One, but I—"

"So am I. It's no trouble, honestly. I'm Charlie Stoker. What's your name?"

"Oh, er, Jennifer, Jennifer Lacey. Thank you, it's very kind of you, but I could have managed it myself."

"It is very heavy, what have you filled it with, house bricks?"

"No, it's all my father's old pharmacy text books." She laughed and relaxed a little. "They are probably no longer suitable for my course, but he insisted on my bringing them. I'll show them to the course teacher and see what he thinks."

"Okay, but you're doing physics. Are the books for the college library?"

"No, not at all. I'm studying pharmacy, like my father. We have to study physics as part of our course."

"I see. That's good, I shall be able to get to know you, then. Shall we go in?"

Since Charlie was still holding her father's books in the air as he turned towards the classroom, Jennifer simply held up her hands in mock despair.

"Oh dear, very well. Thank you so much."

They entered to find the room already quite full. Daphne had gone ahead and booked two places near the front. She called to Jennifer, and Charlie, not seeing a space nearby, reluctantly handed her the briefcase. "Will you visit the refreshment room afterwards?" he asked.

"Oh, no. We have another class and then I must get home." She blushed, pleased he had asked, but firm in her refusal.

"That's okay, I'll look out for you at physics tomorrow."

The initial physics session was to be held in a large airy lecture room, more than fifty students attending. The class, taken by the tall, thin-faced Head of Department, Mr J. Nichol, was for all who needed to study physics at first year or intermediate level, whether as a main or secondary subject. Thus, the twenty-four physics degree students were joined by others studying things like geology, pharmacy or chemistry as their main subject.

Charlie found himself a seat at the rear of the class, next to a serious-looking, bespectacled fellow in a dull tweed jacket and dirty brown brogues. Charlie always noticed other people's footwear.

"Hello," he said, "This seat's not booked, is it?"

The other chap shook his head vigorously and reddened slightly without speaking.

"I'm Charlie Stoker, from Hackney." Charlie held out his hand, "Who are you?"

The bespectacled fellow, reddening even more as he accepted the outstretched hand, introduced himself as R-Robert B-Bruce from H-H-H-H-Harringay.

"Pleased to meet you," Charlie said with a disarming grin. "You a starter?"

"N-n-no, s-s-second year m-mechanical engineering d-d-di-ploma. N-Need ph-ph-ph…," he paused momentarily, "ph-ph-ph—"

"Physics," said Charlie without thinking.

Robert Bruce went even darker red, "Y-y-yes, j-just the one y-year though f-for the di-di-ploma."

"My father was an engineer," said Charlie chattily. "He got his degree here, and always said it was the best place. He wanted me to follow him, so I have, but I'm doing physics, not mech. engineering."

Robert Bruce was saved from having to make further conversation by the entrance of the imperious figure of the Head of Department, who swept past them, gown flowing, on his way to the dais at the front of the room. The young man's features faded to a more natural shade and his shoulders sagged with relief as he regained his composure after the strain of the introduction. Robert had just finished a four-year apprenticeship as a motor mechanic, but was undertaking two years study for the Mechanical Engineering Diploma that would make him a qualified engineer.

He hated meeting new people. He hated seeing the change in demeanour that invariably occurred when he spoke to people for the first time. And sometimes for the second time or third time or every time. It made him want to hide away, to be unseen. And yet, once he felt accepted rather than tolerated, if he was able to relax, his stammer became less pronounced and he enjoyed the social contact. He loved conversation—his mother always told people he was a chatterbox, because she knew he could be—and he had a fine singing voice.

In truth, he was coping much better nowadays. This tall fellow, Charlie Stoker, for example, he seemed a friendly, open type, and he had not been in the least put out by the impediment. That was a good sign. Early days, though.

Mr Nolan introduced himself and referred to the complicated make-up of the group, and to the different requirements of their courses. He then explained in great detail the importance of a grounding in classical Newtonian physics for success in the study of any science. He dwelt upon its relevance to each student's area of study and gave an oversight of the aspects they would be studying. Then, as he exhausted each science group's range of interest, he released those students from the class. The mechanical engineering group were the second last to leave, Robert grinning at Charlie as he went out, and whispering: "S-see you next time."

The department head then outlined the studies the degree physics students would be undertaking in addition to the shared subjects. They would be dealing with heat and the passage of electricity through gases, and they would delve into the new theories of quantum mechanics and relativity, which, in explaining the link between space and time, were changing scientists' view of the universe. These they would be touching upon in their final year studies.

Charlie cycled home quite slowly, thinking about his first day at the Northern and excited about the curriculum. He was not in the least apprehensive about the studies ahead of him. He could see that physics covered a vast field, much of which could be of value in the future, whatever he chose to do with his life.

But what did he really want? Research in a lab? He could not bear the thought of being a teacher in a classroom, something his mother had often suggested. Nor engineering, really. It was messy. Although, he enjoyed working things out and was good with his hands. He had always enjoyed being in the kitchen with his mother or Florrie, baking and preparing food. Maybe he could concentrate on the physics of food processing? Or he could study to become an accountant, of course. That might be interesting. He really liked maths, but it meant being stuck in an office, didn't it? Building the shoe business would be much more exciting than any of these things, really... He'd have to have another talk with his mother.

Chapter Five
Millie and Charlie

Although by her own strength of character and the power of Father Peter's faith and love Millie had regained a raison d'être, she had nevertheless continued to live with an inner emptiness since *that* day. Her raison d'être was, of course, young Charlie, the only person left in the world for her to love and to care for—and to be loved by? She wondered if that were true. Showing love was something that had never come easily to Millie Cowper, and now she was recognising that Charlie was as much of her Cowper blood as of Stoker.

In the two years that had passed since *that* day, there had been closer contact between them than for a long time, and, on the whole, they were getting along quite well. Yet, there was never total ease.

As a mother, she had already much to be proud of in her son. He had been a delightful child with a sunny disposition and an eagerness to hold the floor no matter who should be his audience. As a teenager he had developed into a quiet, intelligent student, popular with his school friends and ever willing to be of assistance at home.

But their personal relationship, the direct link between mother and son, had become cool over the years. Indeed, at times it was quite distant, in contrast to that between the two males of the family, who had grown ever closer to each other until *that* day.

Charles had always indulged his love for their son, even through the years of pain. He would sit down there, stiffly upright on his stool for as long as the youngster wanted to stay, never indicating in any way how much he was suffering and needed to rest. But that was Charles. His warmth had always filled rooms: he had been so full of love, of life and of giving. He had silenced her objections with just a hint of a smile and a slight movement of his shoulders.

Before she met Charles, she had been content to be a good bank clerk: capable, organised, neat, and at all times self-contained. She had never felt any particular sexual attraction to another person, nor sexual need. And then he had burst into her life. Charles was the only person in her whole life to whom she had willingly yielded, intellectually, emotionally and totally. Only Charles had been capable of making her blush with a mere shrug; capable of stirring a passion within her that she had not believed possible.

"Oh, Lord" she murmured, as so many times before, "why did you take him from me?"

But Charles was gone. Now she must be the support for Charlie. Charles had been a quiet man, but a remarkable man. Now, as their son grew closer to the age his father had been when he had first stepped inside her bank, she tried to assess their boy objectively. Young Charlie had much the same build or would have in a few years' time when he filled out a little. He had the same blond hair and even the same winning smile. Yet there was a difference.

There had always been an openness about Charles Stoker; it had been as if one could see straight to his heart. With young Charlie it was not so. Nowadays, she could rarely see beyond those deep blue eyes. They seemed to contain a lock-out mechanism that only allowed through what he chose.

Although, just occasionally, she witnessed a sort of uncertainty that made her want to hug him, to make him feel loved. But hugging was not what Millie did. Cowpers did not hug, they shook hands politely or allowed their cheeks to be pecked; and if Charlie was half Cowper, Millie was all Cowper. A pecked cheek was all she had expected or received for years, except in the front room after *that* day, and even then she had not been able to bring herself to respond to his gesture. She had slammed the door on his attempt to break the barrier.

Millie finished recording the couple of invoices received from Billy's suppliers that morning, closed the day book and placed it in its drawer inside the small chest in her bedroom. It was time to prepare the evening meal for the two of them. Charlie was a youth of seventeen. He would be starving when he had cycled home after his first day at The Northern Polytechnic Institute.

She made her way down the back stairs to the kitchen and lit the gas under the saucepan of peeled potatoes prepared by Florrie before she left for the day. She went through the kitchen door and down the four steps to the garden, where she pulled a fresh cabbage from her vegetable plot to take into the house as an accompaniment for the liver and mash.

Tending the vegetables in the garden was a duty of love for Millie. The small, well-ordered plot provided a haven of peace, an atmosphere devoid of tension. It was a tiny world untouched by the cruelties and sadness of life elsewhere. In her miserable experience, people lived and died with heartbreaking suddenness, and were gone for ever. But her flowers and vegetables returned to her year after year: to bloom in the sun and provide colour, food and joy; to fade in the autumn, certain of return the following spring.

Strangely, it had been a world that Charles never inhabited. On their first arrival in the house in 1910 he had said, "The garden is yours, Millie, my little love, I shall enter it only on your explicit command." Had that remarkable husband of hers always known that she needed this special place to herself, this place where she could uncoil the tight spring within her?

Her musings were interrupted by the sound of Charlie announcing his homecoming in the usual way, slamming the front door and tramping heavily to his room. She returned to the kitchen, smiling to herself. The daily clatter was a comfort. Her son was safely home.

She turned back to the preparation of the evening meal. Liver and onions had always been a family favourite and a weekly staple in the Stoker household. It would please the young man of the house tonight.

* * *

As he devoured his liver and onions at the kitchen table, Charlie related snippets of information about his first day at the Northern. His mother listened in attentive silence. His casual observations reminded her of Charles in the early days of their relationship, with the same sharpness of perception and lack of any criticism or malice. It was, she thought an attribute that would stand him in good stead throughout life.

When Charlie mentioned Arthur Biskin and his respectful comments about Charles and *that* day, she responded in pleasant surprise.

"Mr Biskin? He's a very decent chap, that. It's a nice family, the Biskins. It was his daughter, Sally, who first recognised your father *that* day, you know? She works at the Home and Colonial in Kingsland Road."

"Oh, Sally at the grocer's? Yeah, I know Sally, but I didn't know that. She's never said anything when I've seen her. Mind you, she never talks much, does she? Not like her dad."

"No, she's a quiet girl. I think she takes more after her mother. Mrs Biskin is a mousey little woman, always has her head down. Did you meet anyone else that we know?"

"No, but something Mr Biskin said upset me a bit."

"Oh? What was that?"

"Well, when he said what he did about Dad, he went on a bit about the General Strike. He said most men didn't want it, but then he said you have to see the strikers' point of view. Like, as if he was saying it didn't matter if people got killed in their riots because the fight for all their jobs was worth more than someone's life. That's not right, is it?"

"No, Charlie, that's not right, but Arthur Biskin did not mean it like that. He would never link your father's accident with the strikers' motives. The tragedy happened in that place on that day, but it could have been a sudden surge in any crowd at any time. It was the will of the Lord that your father's misery should end at that time. We cannot begin to comprehend the will of the Lord."

Charlie's eyes narrowed. He sat for some seconds, knife and fork in the air above his plate as he considered his mother's words. Then he continued eating without further comment.

Eventually, Millie prompted him: "Who else did you meet?"

"No one I knew. Met a good-looking girl, though. Very smartly dressed, I must say. I think we were the smartest two people in the college. Most of the students were in overalls or scruffy jackets and woollen ties. I felt out of place, you know what I mean?"

Millie looked at her son very seriously.

"You're never out of place for being well-dressed, Charlie. You may stand out a little, as the young lady did, but you only ever create respect by the standards you set in these things. Tell me more about the young lady."

"There's nothing else, really. We only spoke for a second or two before the afternoon class, then we got separated in the rush. She's studying pharmacy. I'll see her tomorrow, probably. This liver's good, Mum."

Millie averted her head to hide her smile at the sudden change of subject. She was also very conscious of her son's use of the affectionate word 'mum'. It was the familiar term she had grown up with, had always used to her mother, and which Charlie had for some years shied away from, always using the more formal 'mother'.

Neither spoke again until their plates were empty. Charlie's was replaced with a large dish of treacle sponge and custard that disappeared faster than had the liver. For herself, Millie peeled a freshly picked russet apple. There was little further conversation, but the silence was warm and comfortable. After the meal, Charlie rose from the table, intending to study his course paperwork in his room. Millie said:

"So, are you really looking forward to the academic year, Charlie?"

For a moment or two the young man stood, saying nothing. Then he took a deep breath.

"Honestly? Yes, I am. I want to complete my dad's course, Mum, but to tell the truth, I don't know what good it will do me afterwards. I don't want to be a physics teacher, and I don't want to be an engineer. I want to build our shoe business!"

The words rushed out and he blushed, not sure what her reaction would be; but Millie was not seeking confrontation. She looked at him steadily.

"I know that's what you want, son. But let's take one step at a time. Don't worry about the subjects, it's completing the course that matters. For the next two or three years you have to concentrate on finishing your education. Whatever happens after that, you will have the security of the degree, and that will protect you, whatever you do, no matter what winds blow through your life. The shoe business may be the future and it may not. Either way, you will have a future."

Charlie gazed at the little woman who was his mother. As so many times before, he was nonplussed by her calmness and her wisdom.

* * *

The pattern of daily life now began to change for the Stokers of Amhurst Road. As the first academic year progressed, young Charlie was finding life as a student great fun. Academically, with all his exemptions he was free to enjoy an easy year, but he now had a social life as well as an academic life. In addition to his continuing membership of the cycling club, he became a member of the North London Camera Club and the Highgate Swimming Club. He also joined the Amateur Dramatic Society, the Choral Society and the Operatic Society.

In truth, these memberships were mostly bogus. He did not sing, nor did he see himself as an actor; but, according to Jennifer Lacey, his guide and mentor in these matters, he was required to join. He would be needed as a stage-shifter for the Operatic Society when they performed *The Gondoliers* in the spring, in which she was to play the part of Tessa. He would be of invaluable help as a prompter for the Dramatic Society. And of course he would join the debating society and attend the music lectures of the Orchestral Society in the Great Hall, wouldn't he? Charlie had just shrugged and agreed to everything.

Membership of the camera and swimming clubs was a different matter. Swimming, he regarded, like cycling, as good exercise, and he enthusiastically attended the Highgate Club each Saturday. The fascination with photography and cameras probably grew from his vague knowledge of his father's war career.

Charles had always been reluctant to talk about precisely what he did in the war. He had been a technical instructor and a pilot. Any further inquiry generally created an uncomfortable silence. But Charlie remembered the way he had explained the finer points of photography to his mother when she had difficulties with her little Kodak.

The North London Camera Club held its meetings at the Northern Polytechnic Institute. Jennifer was a keen photographer and had been a member the previous year while working in her father's chemist's shop. She had no hesitation in paying the 7s 6d annual subscription to renew her membership.

When Charlie expressed interest, she assured him that it would be well worth the money. There would be lectures, presentations, demonstrations, competitions, and outings. It was all jolly good fun. There was even special tuition for beginners if that were needed.

Charlie explained that he understood how photography worked, but he had no experience of clubs and stuff. Jennifer just laughed and said he would love it. Charlie shrugged, much as he had when signing for the Operatic Society, the Dramatic Society and the Choral Society.

The greatest change to Charlie Stoker's young life, however, came from student social gatherings in the ABC tea rooms or the local public houses. He discovered that he liked beer and he enjoyed smoking cigarettes. He also marvelled to himself at how different the company of young ladies was from his contacts with young girls in former years. Whereas he had always found himself readily accepted into any company, the need for special relationships had never arisen. Now, he found he was very keen to spend time with one lady in particular, the same Miss Jennifer Lacey.

There was something special about Jennifer. She was no more than five feet three inches tall, slim, but with a clearly defined and eye-catching figure, and, as Charlie realised when he stared at her unashamedly, she had shapely legs and ankles—a bit like his mother. They had become friends after that first meeting on the opening day, and Charlie had soon allowed himself to be persuaded into a string of memberships he would never have dreamed of considering otherwise.

Robert Bruce, who had soon become Bobby, joyfully reminded him, whenever the opportunity arose, that it was "c-clear" she had only to give him that "c-c-coquettish" smile and he was "p-p-putty" in her hands. Charlie would just laugh and shrug.

He and Bobby had become good pals since the beginning of the academic year. Bobby had appreciated Charlie's total disregard of his speech impediment, and quickly relaxed in his company. Charlie recognised in Bobby a kindred spirit. Once the stammer was under control, his down-to-earth approach to life and his sharp wit became apparent. They shared a few classes during the week and had other interests in common. Bobby introduced Charlie to the swimming club and Charlie reciprocated by taking Bobby on a cycling trip. Each became a member of the other's club.

With regard to Jennifer, the truth was actually quite the opposite of Bobby's suggestion. It was the lady whose head had been turned. She had never quite recovered from that very first look in the refreshment room when her heart had leapt.

Thereafter, Charlie had become a major factor in her thinking. The only class they shared was the Wednesday afternoon physics class, but they and about eight or ten other students had casually formed a lunch gang that assembled in the refreshment room two or three times per week, and in the saloon of the Victoria Tavern every Friday evening. It was at these times she liked to show off her prize.

The Friday evening gatherings were the highlight of the week. The engineering department of the college included studies in music trades, and there were a number of keen students and competent musicians. On Friday evenings, Magdalena Badicka, a Polish lecturer, piano tuner, and accomplished pianist of indeterminate age, played the piano in the saloon bar of the Victoria Tavern, just fifty yards along the road. As a consequence, the Victoria Tavern became a great attraction and social venue for many students.

Each week, about forty regulars crowded the high-backed, upholstered bench that ran the length of the lounge, and the wooden chairs scattered around the small, polished wood tables. These filled most of the room, and the remaining space was taken by the tiny bar and an upright piano.

Once ensconced, the clientele would hold forth: to argue about whatever was the topic of the day and to discuss the week's events. They could also devour, alone or shared between two or three of them, the home-made pork pies cooked by the wife of the innkeeper; or nibble at a packet of Smith's crisps with its little blue bag of salt. Plates and glasses would clutter the tables, closely watched by the hard-working Jasper, whose task it was to take any repeat orders, to remove the empties and to wipe the tables.

On his first visit, guided by Bobby, an experienced drinker, Charlie sipped at a half-pint of brown ale. Thereafter, that quickly became a pint, then two pints as he developed a taste for it. The air would become thick with the aroma of the food, the fumes of the alcohol, and the smoke from the life-style craze of the twenties, cigarettes.

As soon as Mme Badicka struck a chord on the old upright piano, however, the saloon bar fell silent. Not a sound would be heard during the time it took for her to perform a Chopin piece of her choice. Then the room would erupt in applause until she played an encore, or two, or even three, to screaming approbation. The whole performance rarely lasted for much more than about thirty minutes, after which the artist would disappear silently through a door by the bar. Then, everyone resumed their conversations as if nothing had happened, and for the rest of the evening a little bald-headed man played requests for people to sing along to.

Throughout the evening, Jennifer and Daphne would sit smoking cork-tipped cigarettes and audaciously nursing single glasses of gin and orange. Jennifer liked to attract attention, adopting poses with a long, slender cigarette-holder, blowing clouds of smoke into the air and continually flapping it away from her face. Daphne tended to shy away from contact with other people, and sat hidden in the corner, conducting whispered conversations, mostly with her friend's back.

Charlie had been brought up in a quiet, often sombre household, where the only smoker had been his pipe-smoking grandfather George. The smell of that pipe had been a constant irritation to his mother throughout Charlie's childhood, and she had never permitted its use anywhere in the home beyond the shoe-repair shop.

Neither of his parents had ever smoked, as far as he could remember, and the only consumable alcohol had been kept locked in a small cupboard beneath the big bench in the workshop. It was, the boy had always accepted, a necessary part of his father's medication. He understood that other people imbibed for pleasure, but it had never been the way of things at Amhurst Road. Millie Stoker approved of neither alcohol nor tobacco.

Jennifer came from a quite different background. Her father, the chemist, was rarely seen without a cigarette dangling from the corner of his mouth. It was a habit, he told Charlie at their first meeting, picked up in France in 1915. He found it calming, enabling him to keep his sanity in a field hospital throughout the uproar of war. Charlie, observing him from the wooden chair at the end of the counter, noticed that the energetic little chemist never seemed to drop his ash. He always found time to place it carefully in the ashtray hidden behind the glass-topped counter. Presumably that was a knack also picked up in the field hospital.

It was from Jennifer that Charlie himself gathered the habit of smoking. The new students, eager to make friends, very quickly began to form into groups. Bobby Bruce, Charlie Stoker, Jennifer Lacey and Daphne Hipstead got on well together from the off. Jennifer and Daphne were friends who had been working together in the chemist's shop; Bobby and

Charlie were two exceptionally bright young men who enjoyed each other's company, and that of the two girls.

On fine days, the four sometimes walked to the St Mary Magdalene Gardens at lunch time. Jennifer and Daphne would light their Craven 'A' cork-tipped cigarettes, and Bobby, a Wills' Woodbine. On the third or fourth occasion, as Charlie stood by smiling to himself as he watched the other three lighting and inhaling their chosen smokes, Jennifer proffered her red box. Charlie shook his head firmly. She pressed him but he still declined, saying no, he really didn't ever smoke.

"What, never?" asked a mock incredulous Jennifer in a sing-song voice, quoting from her beloved WS Gilbert.

"No, never!" sang Daphne and Bobby in unison. Both girls burst into peals of laughter and Bobby grinned, but the joke was wasted on Charlie. He just looked at them blankly.

"No," he answered seriously, "No-one smokes at home. My Granddad used to smoke a pipe, but my parents have never smoked."

"You don't know what you're missing, handsome. Here, try a puff of mine," Jennifer coaxed.

Charlie grinned, feeling sheepish; then, rather hesitantly, he took the silver holder from her hand and inhaled slowly. His head flew back as the smoke hit the back of his throat and he began spluttering and choking. Coughing loudly, he thrust the cigarette holder away, wiping his eyes.

"It's damn awful!" he exclaimed to loud laughter from all three of the smokers. Jennifer, laughing loudest, refused to accept the holder from him. The empathetic Bobby said:

"D-do it again, Charlie, b-but don't take such a big gulp. You'll soon get to l-ike it."

Gingerly, Charlie drew on the cigarette a second time, managing to hold himself together and to exhale normally, though conscious of a sensation of light-headedness as he did so. When his head cleared, he inhaled for a third time, this time relaxing and exhaling slowly. "Yeah, I see what you mean," he said, nodding and passing the holder back to Jennifer. "Yeah, it's interesting, the way your head goes fuzzy, isn't it?"

"You're a baby!" cried Jennifer, but Charlie was not in the least disturbed. He shrugged and smiled. Nevertheless, he purchased his first packet of cigarettes the next morning, Player's Medium Navy Cut, as recommended by the tobacconist on the corner of Amhurst Road.

Chapter Six
The Camera Club

The camera club proved to be all that Jennifer had promised. Charlie had become quite adept at using his mother's No. 2 Autographic, and was not at all out of place with the assorted bunch of enthusiasts who had filled room six on the ground floor of the Northern when the club year commenced in October 1928. The first few sessions were most enlightening to new members, being a series of lectures by Mr Whitworth on the history of photography.

Henry Whitworth was a retired physics master from a minor public school in Buckinghamshire. He was the organiser and secretary of the club, a rather nervous, sallow-complexioned man whose hesitantly delivered talks were brilliantly illustrated with slides. There always followed much lively open discussion. A few returning members, including Jennifer, had seen these presentations before, but all were just as enthralled by the mystery and the promise of the world of photography.

The talks illustrated in detail the development of magic lanterns from as far back as the first use of the phenomenon of camera obscura. Mr Whitworth explained how photography had developed from French inventor Joseph Niépce's first permanent photograph in 1827, using a silver-coated plate, through Jacques Daguerre's copper-plated daguerreotypes, to the Eastman-Kodak Brownies that brought photography to millions of homes, and which most of the members were now carrying. Development was still racing ahead. Sophisticated modern cameras such as the Sibyl Excelsior and his own favourite plate camera, the Dallmeyer Speed, were now being used by professionals; and of course the ongoing developments of colour film and the exciting world of cinematography were progressing at breakneck speed.

Other than their interest in the lectures, members were mainly concerned with discussing the basics of taking pictures: learning to remain absolutely still when clicking the camera; to focus properly and to use the light sensibly; not to waste exposures and to save film. They watched demonstrations showing precisely how to do all these things and how to develop their own negatives in dark rooms.

Charlie thoroughly enjoyed all of this, and, as in the lunchtime gatherings or the Friday evening visits to the Victoria, he also derived extraordinary comfort from being with a lot of people with a shared interest, and observing their different personalities and character traits. The club membership was quite large, but a number of members did not attend regularly, attending only on alternate weeks or when the subject matter of the evening's presentation was of particular interest to them. Consequently, it was not until the club's Christmas party that Jennifer introduced Charlie to her long-time friend Margret Mabey.

The two girls had been friends since childhood, their fathers having served together as officers in the Great War. A striking contrast in appearance to the lovely Jennifer, Margret was pale and studious-looking, tall and angular. She had short, tightly-waved black hair, deep-set brown eyes, a narrow nose and thin lips. Nearly a year older than her friend, she was now a student at the London School of Economics. Like Jennifer, a keen photographer, she remained an enthusiastic member of the N.L.C.C. although not a regular attendee.

The Christmas party was held not in the Polytechnic but in the saloon bar of the Victoria Tavern. When Charlie arrived, the party had already commenced. The room was closed off from the rest of the public house and the bar covered with dishes of mince pies, sandwiches, Mrs Potter's home-made pork pies and an iced Christmas cake. He threaded his way through the room to where he knew his friends would be, in the far corner, collecting a mug of beer on the way. By custom, the gentlemen drank beer, and shandies—the same beer diluted with lemonade—were served for the ladies.

This was evidently not a satisfactory arrangement for Margret Mabey, who, spurning the custom, sat in Jennifer's favourite corner seat, wearing a mid-brown, finely-knitted coat-dress, and nursing a pint of beer and a cigarette. Surrounding her were Jennifer herself and a couple of members whose names Charlie did not yet know. Jennifer looked stunning, as ever, in a red dress with a small flower spray pinned to the breast.

Also at the table were Bobby and Daphne—neither of whom were members of the club but had somehow managed to be there. Charlie suspected Jennifer had had something to do with it but he was quite happy to see them. He refrained from comment.

Daphne, it seemed, was now spending as much time with Bobby as with Jennifer, a fact that pleased Charlie, who had begun to see her just as a hanger-on to Jennifer. In Bobby's company, she was blooming: less self-effacing and introverted, and showing a warm personality previously unseen by him.

Bobby jumped up with a big grin and a conspiratorial wink to welcome him.

"Good evening, S-sir Charles, w-welcome. You're late!"

"Cheeky beggar!" retorted Charlie. "Good evening all!"

He sat down in the space saved for him by Jennifer, and was introduced all round. The other two previously unknown members were Walter Hadkin, an earnest-looking man with flappy ears, and Alec Chapman, red-faced and burly, with a moustache. Both knew Jennifer and Margret from the previous year. Margret studied Charlie with an aloof air, then said to Jennifer, "Yes, I see what you mean, quite impressive." Jennifer blushed and giggled, brushing an imaginary hair from her eye.

"Did I interrupt anything?" asked Charlie, sensing a hiatus in the flow of chatter.

"No, not at all. Walter here was just lecturing us about modern developments in photography," replied the moustached chap, Alec Chapman, sarcastically,

"Steady on, old chap, I was simply talking about my work." Walter Hadkin, reddening, was embarrassed to be the centre of attention. He was clearly happier behind a camera than being the focal point of a discussion.

"Well, if it is decided to give a prize for the best photographer, which one of us could win it?" asked Jennifer, rhetorically. "It would have to be you, Walter. You always know what to take, how to get the light right, which settings to use and things like that. And you have the experience of using the best equipment."

"Most of that is just practice, trial and error, and I do get plenty of practice now, working at the Hampstead studio."

"Are you a working photographer then?" asked Charlie.

"Well, I work for a photographer. Mostly, I do the donkey work around the place, but when he is double-booked, I get to do a bit."

"He's being modest, Charlie," insisted Jennifer. "I've seen some of his work, it's beautiful. He's really good."

"Well, last weekend I did get the chance to take a wedding, in colour, working with Autochrome plates," Walter sounded almost apologetic, "but that was unusual. And anyway, you're pretty good yourself, Jen. That field series you did with the butterflies in the summer was terrific. You won the summer competition."

"Yes, but I just got lucky, I simply happened upon them. That was a great day for me."

"But that's what makes a good photographer, spotting the moment."

Jennifer nodded, blushing. "I suppose so, but that's the only one I've ever spotted. Anyway, Margret is better than I am at camera work."

Margret emptied her glass and snorted.

"That's rubbish, Jen. I'm competent, but ordinary, uninspired. You have flair. That's an enviable quality."

Jennifer blushed more deeply.

Mr Whitworth made a short, stumbling address to wish everyone a happy Christmas and to announce a competition for the new season, a single photograph on the theme of 'The Spirit of Winter'. This was greeted with mixed reactions around the room. Bobby said he wasn't sure whether there was any whisky in the house and did that count anyway? Daphne punched him in the arm.

Bobby then became engrossed in a conversation with Alec about motorcycles. Bobby had become wildly interested in motorcycles since his father had purchased a second hand BSA machine, a model L side-valve, only a year old, for ten pounds. It had been badly mistreated but was responding superbly to the care and attention of the budding mechanical engineer. Alec, the 22-year-old son of a local butcher, owned a new AJS M12, bought by his father, he said caustically, to save paying him wages.

The beer was plentiful and Charlie, chatting with the ladies, noticed that Margret's rather aloof air dissipated considerably as the evening progressed. The deep brown eyes softened and the cold features warmed as the steady flow of alcohol warmed her inside. He supposed the same thing was happening to him, but it seemed more natural in a man. He'd never seen a woman drink pints of beer before. Jennifer nursed a single glass of shandy throughout the evening.

A club member had been playing the piano in the corner for part of the evening, pouring out the popular songs of the decade to desultory accompaniment. He began to play *Ol' Man River*, and without warning, Bobby Bruce stood up and sang the lyrics in a fine baritone voice quite free of impediment. The room became hushed until he finished, then there was uproar.

Applause, cheering, stamping and cries of 'More! More!' filled the room. Their table was mobbed with well-wishing members begging for more. The embarrassed Bobby sat down, red as a beetroot and tongue-tied, with a sheepish grin on his face. Daphne, in tears, hugged him.

As the crowd settled down, Mr Whitworth approached the table, an inquiring look on his face. "That was, ah, a beautiful rendering, ah, young man, ah. Forgive me, er… I can't recall your name."

"B-B-B-B-Bruce, sir, B-B-Bobby B-Bruce."

"I see. I don't think we've met before. Are you a new member?"

Jennifer spoke up. "Oh, Mr Whitworth, Bobby is a guest of mine. I forgot to mention it to you."

Whitworth looked unsettled for a moment, then said with a smile: "I see. Well, I suppose that splendid solo effort must pay for one party entrance fee. You have a fine voice, Bobby Bruce. Will you, ah, treat us to another chorus?"

"Y-y-yes sir. Of c-course!"

There was applause again, then silence as the pianist played an introduction and Bobby repeated his performance of the moving *Showboat* song. The musical was that year lighting up London. When the applause died down and the excitement had settled, Daphne said, sighing: "That really is a lovely song, isn't it?"

"Yes, we must all go to see the show before it gets taken off," said Jennifer, looking at Charlie, who smiled and shrugged; but Daphne responded:

"Yes, let's all go as a group, it'll be great fun."

Alec had disappeared by this time, but the rest of the crowd all agreed and Jennifer was charged with obtaining the tickets. The idea was soon forgotten.

"Th-there are a few great songs out this year, aren't there?" mused Bobby to the table at large. No one responded immediately, so he turned to Daphne and sang: "A room with a view—and you..." to which she replied:

"I can't give you anything but love, baby!"

"Oh, will it ever come true, our room with a view?" crooned Bobby.

Daphne, laughing, sang: "Dream awhile, scheme awhile..." and brought the house down.

Chapter Seven
Xmas 1928

Christmas, never a time for wild festivities in the Stoker household, had become very quiet by 1928. Millie had bought Charlie a silver cigarette case as a Christmas present, together with a box of fifty Senior Service cigarettes, his new favourite brand, and an instruction that, in the house, they were to be smoked only in his room with the window open.

Beyond his room, though, life was becoming ever more exciting for the young man. He was eighteen years old and looked older, was fully six feet tall, and handsome. Life was full of hidden promises. There had been, throughout the holiday period, a series of activities and parties that kept him out quite late, but he always tried to be home by midnight. The one occasion he seriously failed to do so was the night he attended a party held by Jennifer at the family home on Highgate Hill, at the end of the week after Xmas.

The house was a similar sized building to the Stoker house in Amhurst Road but was occupied entirely by the Laceys, their four children, of whom Jennifer was the eldest, and a maid. The lower two floors formed the family living area, and the two floors above were bedrooms. Mrs Lacey had taken the three younger children to visit Torquay for a few days, leaving only Mr Lacey and the maid to watch over proceedings. The consequence was a great deal of fun for all involved.

Mr Lacey had a relaxed attitude to life and spent much of the evening acting as the family butler. Everybody was served a large sherry on entry and glasses were rapidly topped up thereafter. A fine buffet accompanied by assorted wines had been laid out, and guests spread themselves about and enjoyed themselves. A large room on the first floor had been cleared for dancing, and a cousin of Jennifer's played the piano. The wine flowed freely and the atmosphere was quickly filled with shouting, singing, laughing, tobacco smoke, and alcohol fumes.

Charlie, a most reluctant dancer, stood near the door of the music room, smilingly watching two or three couples, including Bobby and Daphne, dancing the Charleston enthusiastically. Suddenly, Jennifer, having partaken of two or three glasses of wine, decided to teach him the steps of the dance. She dragged him onto the dance floor and began to lead him round.

Easy-going Charlie, however, was only easy-going until he made a decision. On this occasion he decided that he could not, and would not, dance the Charleston. The futile exercise lasted only a few minutes, at the end of which Jennifer flew into a sudden rage, angrily declared him a stupid imbecile, and flounced off to grab another partner.

Charlie was quite unperturbed. He wandered back down into the dining room where a glass was thrust into his hand by a sympathetic Mr Lacey with the comment, "I don't dance, either."

The chemist was a fascinating character who liked to chat, and the next part of the evening passed delightfully for both of them, the young man being regaled with a mixture of reminiscences and observations, many caustic, on the Great War, while his glass was regularly replenished with whatever his host happened to be pouring. Charlie had begun the evening with a couple of sherries and had also drunk a few glasses of wine, but now, Lionel Lacey had moved him on to his own favourite tipple, Jamieson's Irish whisky.

Since having been introduced to beer by Bobby at the Victoria Tavern and finding he enjoyed it, Charlie had come to look forward to having a few drinks whenever possible. His mother always talked of it as evil, but it had no ill-effects upon him, and he found it exciting to discover the different taste behind every new label. Of course, until this night most of those labels had been ales and stouts. He had sampled a few wines, but had been less than thrilled by them. He had tried gin once, and rum—which he positively disliked—but not whisky. This was a new experience. He loved the dryness and the bite of it; it felt really good.

That is, it felt really good until he needed to relieve himself. Mr Lacey had gone off with the decanters on one of his regular rounds to top people up in the other rooms, so Charlie got up to go to the bathroom. He found his legs suddenly very unsteady. He shook his head in surprise and the room swam around him. With an effort of concentration, he made his way, rocking a little, to the staircase, dragging himself halfway up the second flight before coming to a weaving halt. He leaned on the handrail to steady himself but was having difficulty seeing clearly.

"Here, Big Boy, let me help. Lean on me." A deep female voice spoke the words in a firm tone, and a silken arm went around his waist to support his weaving body. The silk-clad angel half guided and half pushed him up the remaining stairs and through the lavatory door. In a quick movement, she flicked the door closed with her heel as she bent to scoop up the chamber pot from the floor beside the lavatory pedestal, and shove it under Charlie's face. He was struggling unsuccessfully to unbutton his trousers.

"Just hold this," she commanded, "I'll do that!"

The hapless Charlie did as he was told and stood, gripping the chamber pot with both hands, and uttering only a soft grunt as his fly was unbuttoned and his penis gently extracted and directed towards the open lavatory pan.

The operation would have been a complete success had not the tremor building in Charlie's stomach suddenly become a volcanic eruption. The shock made him jerk his rear backwards as he vomited into the chamber pot. The angel's grip was momentarily disturbed, sending urine in an arc over the pan, on to the wall, and, as she staggered to regain control, onto both his woollen trousers and her cream silk suit. But the angel did not flinch. Steadying herself, she told Charlie to remain still until his body completed what it had to do.

He was in no condition to argue, and so they remained until all activity had stopped; then she gently tucked his private parts back into his trousers and wiped down all the surfaces of the small room with the lavatory towel. She removed the pot from Charlie's shaky grip, emptied it into the pan, then flushed and wiped the pan. The chamber pot, she carried into the bathroom next door, cleaned, and returned to the lavatory floor. At the same time she collected a lady's dressing gown from a hook on the bathroom door. Finally, she led him out of the lavatory and along the landing into a large bedroom.

"Now, off with your trousers. Sit on the bed," she instructed. Charlie blinked, but did as he was told, and meekly sat as she pulled them from him. Then he stared in amazement as she casually threw off her own long, loose jacket and quite deliberately unclipped the waist-band of her wide, flowing pyjama pants, allowing them to drop to the floor and to reveal a beautiful pair of long, slender legs.

"I can't think straight. This is all so unreal." Charlie attempted a shrug, but his body just drooped.

"Feeling bad, Big Boy?" asked the angel tenderly. She placed the silk dressing gown around her shoulders and sat down next to him. "It happens to the best of us, my friend. No-one I know has escaped that at some time or other. I had my first bout years ago, and there've been quite a few since." She smiled and stroked his thigh, causing a surprising constriction in his underpants.

A cord was hanging by the bedhead. She reached past him and pulled on it. "You realise I know this household very well. I have stayed here on numerous occasions over many years. Ada, the maid, is a very discreet sweetie. If she is now in the kitchen, as I expect, she will solve our problem. Is your head very bad?"

"I just feel very tired."

"You're lucky if that's all. I always get a stinker of a head, but you should be able to have a sleep in a minute." She patted his arm and smiled. "It looks like you'll get off very lightly for a first offence!"

There was a polite tap on the door, it opened slightly and the maid, Ada, peered round it. Then she nodded knowingly, entered and closed the door behind her. She smiled. "I thought it must be you, Miss, as Miss Jennifer and Mr Lacey are busy downstairs. Is this too much of Mr Lacey's Jamieson's again?"

"You've hit it on the head, Ada. I don't think handsome here knows what's going on, but there's been a bit of an accident, and our trousers have both been swamped. Is it possible for you to disappear with them for a few minutes and do one of your steam and press miracles?"

Ada laughed. "You know I will, Miss. I'll be as quick as I can, but with people all over the place, you'd better lock the door behind me." She took the clothes and hurried out.

"Okay," said the angel, "That won't take too long. Why don't you stretch out and have a little rest? I expect I shall read." She pulled the bedcovers down on one side and rolled Charlie gently into the bed. He tried to catch her hand but missed and his arm fell limply beside him. Then he fell asleep. The angel locked the door and turned off the central light in favour of a small reading lamp.

When Charlie awoke, a slow awakening, the room was dark. He sat up, and was quickly reminded of his situation. His legs were groggy and he was desperately thirsty. He had a headache. It was some minutes before he felt steady enough to walk around the room, but eventually he found the light switch. A small clock sitting on the mantelpiece above the fireplace showed 1.55. Charlie wasn't sure that he'd ever been up this late. His trousers were on a chair by the bed, neatly pressed. There was no sign of the silk-clad angel. He dressed and went along to the bathroom to wash his face and swill his mouth out.

The water tasted good and refreshed him enough that he felt able to go downstairs. Lights were still on but there was no music to be heard in the deserted music room. He carried on down to the lower floor and almost bumped into Mr Lacey, just coming out of the dining room with his arms full of a collection of empty and part-empty bottles.

"Hello, young fellow, I thought you'd gone home with the others. Where were you hiding?" Then, without waiting for an answer, "Are you staying with us tonight? I think the bedrooms are all occupied now, but you could settle comfortably on a sofa with some blankets. Can I get you anything?"

"No thanks, Mr Lacey, that's very generous of you, but I must go home now. I seem to have lost a few hours, I should have been home ages ago. I'll get right away, if you don't mind. My bike is outside."

"Whatever you prefer, old chap, there's plenty of room here, you know."

"You're very kind, sir. I'm sorry, I seem to have missed Jennifer," he glanced around the deserted floor, "I wanted to—" He stopped, not sure what he wanted to say, but it mattered not to Mr Lacey.

"She will be fast asleep by now, but I shall tell her you said goodnight."

The sharp winter air acted as a tonic for Charlie, clearing his head as he rode home reflecting upon the events of the evening—as far as he could recall them. *Everything had gone swimmingly at first*, he thought. Jennifer had been at her most attentive when he arrived, staying close to him and introducing him to her cousins and various friends as if he were a hero. It had been very nice, he acknowledged to himself as he free-wheeled most of the way down the long hill past the Northern Polytechnic Institute and into Highbury.

The buffet had been delicious and he'd enjoyed the sherry and the wine. And so had she, she was at her stunning best, he'd thought. She even took two glasses of sherry. He'd never seen Jennifer take more than a sip of anything before…and she'd had some wine. She had been full of fun and at her most giggly, adorable…until that ridiculous performance on the dance floor.

And that was another first. It really was most odd, the way she had suddenly exploded. He'd never seen Jennifer throw a tantrum before. "A child could do it!" she had screamed at him. She had called him a stupid imbecile. And she had punched him, hard. He had no time for such behaviour, such lack of self-control. He had seen children at school act like that, but it had never concerned him personally before.

He turned onto Balls Pond Road and put the Charleston image out of his mind. Mr Lacey was a strange man, wasn't he? He seemed to let everything go on around him as if he were in a different world; but listening to his stories of the war had been tremendously moving and interesting, and that Jamieson's whisky had been super.

It was what happened after that that Charlie found difficult to sort out. It all became misty in his mind from when he started to go upstairs. He had memories of being violently sick in a chamber pot, a mental picture of an elegant lady in silk, and an unforgettable image of long, slender legs being uncovered in a bedroom. It was ridiculous. And how did he get into that bed? And his trousers had been freshly pressed!

The house was in darkness when he reached home. He removed his shoes and crept into his room, relieved to see his own bed.

* * *

For the rest of the winter break, including welcoming the New Year, Charlie passed the time quietly at home with his mother. He did some studying, and spent a few hours assisting and chatting with Billy Walters in the workshop; but he also sat for considerable periods in his room, trying to correctly put together his confused recollections of the experience at Highgate.

Exactly what had occurred on the night of Jennifer's party remained a mystery to Charlie. The following day, he had made a telephone call to the Lacey's, intending to talk with Jennifer and to clarify the matter, only to be informed—to be reminded—by the maid that Mr Lacey and Jennifer had driven to Torquay to join the rest of the family for the New Year celebrations. Jennifer had, of course, told him weeks earlier of their plans for the holiday period.

He went for a couple of cycle rides, and on the first Saturday of the New Year he met Bobby for their weekly swim. They had missed their sessions through Christmas and were keen to renew the routine.

Charlie, who always appeared older than his eighteen years, enjoyed Bobby's company, and Bobby, the shy stutterer, was making friends and enjoying a busy social life for the first time. He was now nearly twenty years old, having completed his apprenticeship before starting his engineering course. In addition to the Polytechnic, there was his new motorcycle, the clubs he had joined, the cycling, the swimming, and above all, a romance with Daphne that was rapidly becoming serious.

As the two friends sat, nursing glasses of Tizer after their morning swim, they discussed their shared experiences of the holidays and the potential consequences. Bobby explained that he would not have the time for both cycling and motorcycling from now on. He had rather lost his enthusiasm for the bike, he admitted. Charlie just shrugged, and grinned at him. Bobby blushed.

"Y-y-yeah, I s'pose it is more exc-citing to ride the motorbike, es-specially with Daphne holding my waist." He grinned sheepishly and fiddled with his glass.

"Good luck to you, chum, it's fine with me. You seem to have found a little treasure in Daphne, you two look as if you were made for each other. I should hold on tight if I were you."

"Y-you'll still come swimming, won't you, Charlie?"

"O'course I will, I'll always be your friend, Bobby. You're alright, a damned good chap."

"A-and you, Charlie, the v-very best."

Bobby suddenly clasped his friend's arm in a vice-like grip, his face bright red, moist eyes gleaming through his spectacles. "I c-can't believe that I found you and D-Daphne at the same time."

Charlie, the Stoker smile playing around his eyes, sipped his Tizer and shrugged. He cared for Bobby, he realised, in a way he had never experienced before. In this red-headed, stammering, bespectacled motor mechanic he had found a real friend, his first real friend.

"You two looked good dancing the Charleston," he said after some time. "Have you always done dancing?"

"N-no, not much, really. Daphne likes it, and we practiced quite a bit for the p-party, but it's not h-hard, once you do a bit. And after a few drinks, you don't really think about what you're doing. I didn't even know you saw us, I never saw you all evening. It was a good p-arty, wasn't it? I took Daphne home about eleven o'clock, we'd both had a few drinks. You leave early?"

"No, 'fraid not. After Jennifer gave me the push off, I got very drunk on Mr Lacey's Irish whisky. Then I flaked out."

"Y-You w-w-what? J-Jennifer g-gave you the p-push off? I don't believe it. She's mad about you. She's always telling Daphne."

"I think that should be 'was'. She called me a stupid imbecile and went off with someone else. I never saw her again."

"B-b-bloody damn!"

"Yeah, quite. But she threw such a tantrum that I don't think I want to become involved any more. It came as a shock to me, and to be honest I don't want to see it again."

"W-well, I wouldn't be too hasty, old man. I m-ean, that's w-women, isn't it? They do that sort of thing, then the next day they've forgotten all about it."

Charlie pondered that for a minute, then leaned forward and lowered his voice.

"I don't think she'll forget this one too quickly, Bobby. I've been trying to work out what happened that night, but I think I finished the night in Mr Lacey's bed with an unknown woman."

Bobby sagged in his seat, mouth open. "Y-you d-did wh-at?"

"That's the trouble. I just don't know what I did. All I do know is that I woke up in a dark bedroom at half past one and everybody had gone home."

"B-limey, Charlie, that's a b-it of a sh-shaker. D-id anyone see you leave?"

"Oh yeah, Mr Lacey was still up and about. He was quite relaxed about it. He said goodnight, but I don't know what he thought when he got upstairs."

"C-crikey!" Bobby worked through this. "The L-aceys' bedroom? And why do you think you were with a woman?"

Charlie had skated through the first eighteen years of life without any serious emotional crises. He'd had the usual childish squabbles with other youngsters, and his ears had been boxed once or twice by an angry mother, but he had always taken such things in his stride. He had always been a well-behaved and easy-going boy. Nothing had ever really disturbed him. Nothing had made much of a dent in his self-confidence. Not till now. This was different. He was ashamed of what he could not remember, of what sins he may have committed.

He tried to tell Bobby what he could remember of his evening following the scene with Jennifer: listening to Mr Lacey and drinking Jamieson's; the room going round and round; dragging himself up the stairs. Then it all became fantastic…vomiting into a chamber pot—that memory was crystal clear—and with someone holding his penis! Yes, really! And no, he hadn't a clue who it was or what happened next.

The fragmented pictures in his mind portrayed, again and again, blurred images of the angel in cream silk, and of the shedding of her garments—a film star's luxurious silk trousers falling away from long, shapely legs… and her smile, fading into blackness. Trying to clarify the images was like looking through a twisted mirror. What he saw was ever changing, ever distorted; always different and always incomprehensible.

Charlie being Charlie though, the painful memory of the night at Highgate faded from his consciousness after a few more days. Bobby had offered little more in comment than "B-b-bloody damn!" and a conviction that all would be alright with Jennifer when she returned from Torquay.

But Charlie did not care too much about what Jennifer thought. In his assessment of the matter, she had behaved appallingly. Any residual embarrassment about his own behaviour lay in his inability to recall who had been his caring angel, and in the unauthorised use of the master bedroom.

Chapter Eight
Stephen Collick

The year 1929 is remembered by historians principally for the Wall Street Crash and the beginning of the Great Depression. But throughout the year newspapers had been carrying many dark stories of global troubles: religious riots in India; running battles between communists and police in Berlin; fascism in what was now Mussolini's Italy; and fearful times in Ireland, where the authorities were obliged to release the gaoled Irish Nationalist leader De Valera silently through the back door of the gaol to avoid a demonstration by his sympathisers.

In England, although Londoners generally had fared less badly throughout the long, difficult post-war period than the industrial workers of the midlands and the north, the outlook was bleak everywhere. It was, for most people, simply another year of belt-tightening, of working ever harder for smaller returns. Unemployment had reached fifteen percent and was still rising. The general election in May ended in a stalemate, with the Conservatives polling more votes than the opposition, but Labour gaining more seats. In June, Ramsay MacDonald, promising jobs for the unemployed, was to form the new Labour government with Margaret Bondfield, the first ever woman cabinet minister, as his Minister of labour.

For Millie Stoker, though, the turn of the year meant just another winter of time passing, of living half a life: life without her beloved Charles. Each day she followed her daily routines. She had had a telephone installed in the house in order to better attend to Billy Walters' needs in the shoe repair shop. She cared for her son Charlie. She dealt with her tenant's queries and problems. She went on her usual shopping rounds. She chatted to Florrie and went through the motions of a normal life, and, every Sunday, without fail, she placed flowers on her husband's grave and knelt there to be near him.

The New Year had been welcomed by the Stokers in the company of Father Peter and a number of friends from the congregation at the church in Bouverie Road. A grand new church was being built next to the old iron building that had served for forty years; but while parts were now completed, construction was ongoing, and in the meantime the old church continued to provide a facility for the members. For mother and son it was a comforting and non-taxing way to celebrate the occasion, and both enjoyed the peaceful atmosphere and the company.

The warmth and bright colours of spring eventually chased away winter, only for the month of May to bring the anniversary of *that* day and the rekindling of her burning grief.

Dear Father Peter was the only person who ever heard an audible expression of Millie Stoker's enduring misery in those early years after Charles's death. Each week, the old priest dutifully sat and listened as she reiterated her tear-driven confessions, her sins of self-pity. Each week they prayed for God's forgiveness for her sins, and for some contentment in life henceforth; although the latter was a prayer perhaps made even more fervently by the priest when alone in his private quarters, alone with his feelings of inadequacy and a bottle of whisky.

The service of remembrance for Charles had been held on the third Sunday in June, and each year on that day she placed extra flowers on the well-tended plot. In 1929, the weather was fine and a number of people were moving around the burial grounds quite early. Nevertheless, Millie was surprised to find someone standing at Charles's graveside when she arrived there. More intriguing still, she recognised the slim, rather elegant figure of the Hon. Stephen Collick.

Mr Collick turned to greet her, smiling his sad-faced smile, "Mrs Stoker, please forgive me, an intruder in this sacred space. I stayed at my club in town last night and could not pass through without paying my respects to your late husband, my dear friend Charles."

"I am pleased to see you here, Mr Collick, if a bit surprised. I don't expect anyone else to remember the significance of this day."

Millie put forward her free hand to meet his outstretched arm, and he immediately grasped it and pressed it gently between his two large hands.

"Oh, call me Stephen, please, Ma'am. I never forget this date. I have visited Charles each year on this date, and on many other occasions, but usually during the afternoons rather than in the morning, as today. Indeed, for the first few visits my uncle came too, but his health is failing and he rarely leaves the estate now."

He reluctantly released her hand, and continued: "But how are you? Are you and your son keeping well? Are you managing your affairs well enough? You know, I meant every word of my promise to you, but I have received no call and have not dared to intrude upon your privacy. I hope I have not been remiss."

The courteous gentleman stopped speaking, and stood looking anxiously at Millie, more like a loyal servant than the son of a baron.

"Oh, Mr—er, Stephen," she replied, blushing at the use of his first name, "I assure you there has been no need. In no respect have you failed in your duty. Your, and your family's, generosity has been like a gift from the Lord to young Charlie and myself. In these sad and difficult times we have been financially comfortable, and we owe that to you. I feel nothing but gratitude for your actions."

Millie excused herself so that she could arrange the flowers around Charles's grave and tidy up the area. She felt embarrassed by Collick's very proper, old-fashioned, manner of address. He stepped back to give her room to work but made no attempt to leave. When she finished, he leapt forward again to help her up, then said, in the serious tone she was beginning to recognise as normal for him:

"Mrs Stoker, I acknowledge that the Estate have been benefactors to Charles's family, but that was an obligation fulfilled. I sincerely wish to go further. You may recall that, three years ago, I said I would consider it an honour to be regarded as a friend. May I now repeat that as a request? Would you allow me to be your friend and to maintain contact with you?"

Millie did not reply at once. She masked her embarrassment by busying herself in ensuring she was free from soil and ready for church and Father Peter. Then, regaining her composure, she said: "The honour, Mr Coll—Stephen, the honour would be mine; and please call me Millie. Would you care to join me for tea this afternoon?"

"I can think of nothing I should enjoy more, dear Millie, but today I am committed to returning to Epping. However, if you have no arrangement for next Sunday, I should be honoured if you would allow me to take you for a drive. I could collect you at, say, 2.00 pm, if that suits you, and we can drive through the country and enjoy afternoon tea together at the Westcliff Hotel. What do you say?"

"I say yes, Stephen. That will be lovely, I shall look forward to it immensely."

* * *

At precisely 2.00 pm on a gloriously bright Sunday afternoon, Millie, dressed in a rather formal yellow crêpe de Chine frock and a brimmed white Manila hat with a matching yellow ribbon, saw from her peeping position behind the curtains in the front room, a shining red Lanchester saloon with a black roof roll to a stop outside the house in Amhurst Road. Stephen Collick emerged cautiously from the motor car and walked hesitantly up the seven steps to the front door to rap the brass knocker.

She slipped on the afternoon coat she had bought specially for the occasion and opened the door.

"To the minute, sir, admirable." She greeted him with a smile.

"I should not have dared be late for this afternoon, Ma'am," replied Collick, his nervous smile betraying his anxiety. "In truth, I have been waiting along the road for some time to ensure my timeliness."

"I'm happy to see you, Stephen," she emphasised his name. "What a beautiful afternoon you chose!"

"And I am delighted to see you, Millie." His smile became more relaxed. "Yes, it is a lovely afternoon, we shall have a pretty drive today. Allow me."

He ushered her towards the car, backing down the steps and opening the rear door. Millie sat down in the lush comfort of the saloon, struck by the luxury and the strong smell of new leather. The smell reminded her of her old manager's office, but here it was far more intense.

Stephen Collick ensured she was settled, then busily arranged himself in the driver's seat and called over his shoulder: "All comfortable? Good, here we go. Have you travelled on the new arterial roads before?"

"Ah, no. It is several years since we have been on outings, and then they were usually to the West End, to the parks and the museums. On the few occasions we made the trip to Leigh-on Sea or to Southend, it was always in the railway train. This is my first proper drive in a luxury motor car."

Stephen Collick beamed. "Then this is doubly an honour for me. We shall take the northern arterial outward via Eastern Avenue and return by the southern route through Pitsea, nearer to the river."

He pulled at the shiny walnut starter knob. The engine spluttered, kicked into life and settled to a pleasant purr. They were off.

Millie quickly grew accustomed to the gentle up and down movements of the Lanchester's suspension as the car travelled over the bumpy roads across Hackney marshes and through Leytonstone to Whipps Cross and the big main road east to Southend. Once on Eastern Avenue and then the Arterial with its new surface, the ride became much smoother and seductively comfortable.

She found it surprisingly peaceful watching the world go by: first, the big detached or semi-detached houses, standing or under construction well back from the sides of the main road; and then, as they left the fast-growing areas of the city suburbs, the green fields and hedgerows full of summer growth and colour. She saw sheep, cattle and horses grazing in pastures between the fields of crops, each animal seemingly only aware of the patch it occupied and blissfully ignorant of the strange, noisy creatures passing by on the other side of the hedge.

Stephen Collick concentrated upon his driving, and conversation between them was no more than desultory; but he called out to her at intervals, indicating points of interest he considered worth noticing or just voicing casual observations. The journey to the coast lasted more than an hour, but ended far too soon for Millie. It was, for her, an experience to treasure.

They drew to a halt outside the Westcliff Hotel, where Mr Collick was welcomed as a known and respected patron by the top-hatted hotel concierge in his red coat. He ushered them towards the terraced restaurant, where the maître d'hôtel, fawning, led them to the best table in the room for afternoon tea.

The table, already set for two, was by the opened window of the glass-roofed terrace, with a magnificent view over the bustling promenade and the crowded pebble beach where happy bathers splashed in the sea. It was high tide, the sun was shining brightly and the sea was a shimmering, silver-blue vista distantly spotted with the small boats of the local fishermen, bobbing gently up and down below the cloudless sky.

Silver platters appeared, filling the dazzling white cloth surface with fingers of sandwiches, glazed scones with clotted cream and jam, and sweet pastries and cakes. Tea was poured for them. Stephen Collick, very aware of the impression made upon Millie, settled himself and looked across the table at her.

"I noticed, Millie, dear lady, from my glances through the rear-view mirror as we drove here, that you were absorbed by all that you saw from the window on the journey. Now, I assure you, you are about to enjoy the best afternoon tea east of London!"

"Oh, Stephen, I have never been on such a luxurious trip. You have a beautiful motorcar and it was a thrill to travel in it. Thank you for doing this."

Collick, always easily embarrassed, smiled shyly. "It is nothing, I assure you. It gives me more pleasure than you can imagine to be here with you, Millie."

They enjoyed the food and tea for a short time, then he wiped his mouth with his napkin and adopted a more serious look.

"Indeed, I have been a coward for so long," he said. "I have needed to talk with you and to spend time with you for so many years. I always refrained from visiting because I have honoured Charles's decree until now. You yourself nursed him for eight years, and now he has been dead for more than three years. I think that is enough punishment for my crime."

Millie lifted her head sharply. "Crime? What crime? I don't understand what you are talking about."

This was not what she had expected.

Collick sighed.

"Millie, I shall try to explain everything as well as I can. The story goes back to before the war. Charles and I were the same age and came into the works at the same time. We quickly came to respect each other and to like each other. In fact, the longer I knew Charles the more I admired him and the fonder I became of him."

"You knew, of course, that your husband was a brilliant engineer and had become a key figure in the printing company. He had proven himself a genius at keeping the machinery working, and in constantly developing improvements. In fact, his powers of innovation and invention were quite startling to my family.

"After about 1912, he introduced a new method of using photography in printing and some other inventions that I never quite understood. But that is of no import. My contribution was always on the legal and financial needs of the business. My uncle, the Major General, however, was quick to see a potential value to the army in Charles's work, and the consequent enormous value to the company of any such development."

"Sir Arthur had very strong links to the Royal Flying Corps through his long-standing friendship with its commanding officer, Brigadier-General Sir David Henderson.

In 1914, he used his contacts to negotiate an arrangement whereby we would develop a similar process for the armed forces. This was, of course, very hush-hush work and Charles was sworn to secrecy and was required to sign the Official Secrets Act."

"It also meant that he would need to be based at Farnborough to supervise the adaptation of his photographic systems for use in aircraft for aerial photography, while also overseeing the installation of his other developments in other military situations.

"Charles himself suggested that since he was eager to serve his country, perhaps he should be recruited into the Royal Flying Corps. This would also enable him to comprehend more fully all aspects of the operations from the point of view of the people performing them. This was arranged and after a period of training he was quickly promoted to Captain.

"Because of the legal and financial ramifications of the business enterprise, I worked closely with Charles throughout this period, spending a considerable amount of time liaising between Farnborough and Clerkenwell until the end of 1914. I watched him at work, Millie. He was a remarkable teacher and a natural leader. I admired him immensely."

He paused, drank some tea, and sighed. Millie sat, still as stone, but with her mind whirling around the questions she suspected may at last be being answered.

"You will remember, at the memorial service three years ago," said Stephen Collick, resuming his story, "that I said that your husband was a hero. Charles was sent to Farnborough as an engineer instructor. As it became clear what was happening in France at the beginning of 1915, he insisted on becoming a pilot. He was determined to show by example what could be achieved with the new equipment and the proposed methods of use he had introduced. Also he would discover how to make further developments from what he learned in action."

"Of course, the potential financial gain to the war effort was tremendous, to say nothing of the gain to the company and to the estate. We all encouraged him shamelessly. Charles went off to France with his squadron and inspired them to do some remarkable work in photographic reconnaissance, to say nothing of the part he played in keeping up the spirits of inexperienced young pilots. They flew daily, not knowing whether they would live to see any tomorrow, which so many of them tragically did not. The aircraft they flew, the B.E.2 in its various models, was remarkably steady and stable in flight, ideal for photographic work, but also, sadly, an easy target for German fighters."

"Charles was supposed to be strictly non-combatant. He had been instructed not to fly near the battle lines, and was restricted to training flights in safer airspace. I am convinced, though, that the constant strain of losing aircraft and of losing fliers deeply affected him. I believe that he decided it was essential to his work to experience personally what they were going through every day. To that end, he planned a vital mission."

"When, in carrying out that mission, Charles was shot down, he had acquired detailed information about unknown German installations. Somehow, he managed to glide his damaged plane to safe territory before bringing it down in such a way as to save both his equipment and the pictures he had captured. It was an endeavour of astonishing brilliance and bravery."

"My uncle, the Major General, immediately recommended him for the Military Cross for valour. This request was blocked, however, when it was established that he had been flying alone. Flying solo with cameras was strictly against orders, and an unnamed officer on the administrative staff had reported the fact. You will understand, I am sure, that in the army orders are orders. Instead of a Military Cross, army procedure dictated a court martial for recklessly causing the loss of an aircraft."

"Such a catastrophe was prevented by direct order of the Brigadier General himself. Instead, Charles was granted an honourable discharge from the service with a Silver War Badge with King's Certificate, as issued to all service personnel discharged due to wounds or sickness during the war. His heroism was deliberately unacknowledged. Somewhat ironic, eh?"

Stephen Collick's face was the colour of ash when he finished speaking. He sagged in the chair and fiddled with his napkin. Cakes sat on platters and cold tea lay in half-empty cups. The sun still shone brightly and all the seaside activity outside the window continued unabated.

Millie made no immediate move to speak, but a single tear rolled down her face. She allowed it to run its course onto the collar of her yellow dress.

"You have answered many unasked questions, Stephen," she said at last. "I am sad that I have remained in ignorance of the truth for all this time. Yet the picture you paint is one that I recognise. My husband was a very special man who always showed a light face to the world. He sought and thrived on challenges. He could never accept failure in himself. No matter how others saw it, I realise, now, that he regarded that air crash as his personal failure, and he carried the weight and the pain of the consequences for the rest of his life."

She paused to dab at her damp eye with her napkin, then said, "You see, I have at home a short letter I received in March 1917 from France. In it, Charles told me that he had wrecked an aircraft and that he would be home soon. But it was written in a frivolous, ironic style that was quite unlike him. There was the faintest hint of bitterness in the last line, but even that could be interpreted as mere exasperation. Only today have I fully understood its meaning."

A second tear found its way down her cheek. Stephen Collick nodded sadly.

"Yes, I can believe that, dear Millie. But you do understand, don't you, that not only did the war effort gain from the information he recorded on that mission; the whole world—with the exception of Charles himself, and you and your son—we all benefitted hugely from all his endeavours."

"The country gained, with aerial photography having been advanced massively and the armed services becoming far better equipped. The printing industry gained enormously, adopting the technical developments Charles had introduced.

As for the Collick Estate, we reaped vast rewards from sales of military equipment to the government and from the development of the subsequent commercial potential."

"Meantime, that brilliant, broken man blocked out everything from his mind except what he saw as a failure, the self-inflicted end to his career; and his family's welfare, which he, and only he, must be allowed to care for."

He took a deep breath.

"Millie, I failed my friend Charles in 1918. I was not able to be near when he needed me. I was attached to the army in Palestine and by the time I returned, after the battle of Megiddo, it was all over. Charles had set his own path and bluntly refused all our attempts to make recompense."

"He was a fine man, Millie, but an extremely stubborn one. He said I was not to contact him or his family. He said he was not worthy of my friendship and he must find his own way to salvation. They were his exact words. I was shut out and I have never been able to accept his rejection."

Millie tried to absorb, to rationalise, all that she had been told; and to tick off in her mind the answers to all those questions that had plagued her since their conversation at the memorial service. There was one that remained unanswered, and she attempted to raise it tactfully.

"Stephen, what you have done this afternoon must have taken an immense amount of courage. I shall never be able to thank you enough for your openness and your honesty. You have lifted a personal weight of guilt from my shoulders that at times has been unbearable. I can now, at last, move on with my life."

"You still appear to believe, though, that your family was the cause of Charles's troubles. That is not so. Charles did what he believed to be right at all times. He needed to enlist in the army. He saw it as his duty. Your family simply opened a route for him to do what he wanted to do. Gaining advantage for his future career was a bonus, not a purpose."

"The tragedy of the accident and its consequences is something different. Charles would never deliberately break the law or the rules. Whatever the truth of that last photographic expedition, the one certainty is that Charles thought he was doing the right thing. I know he would not care a fig about receiving a Military Cross, but one outcome he could never have visualised was to be threatened with the shame of a court martial. That would have been a dagger to his heart. Charles was the most honest, proud and upright man in the world."

Millie faltered for a moment, then recovered.

"The only question still unresolved for me," she said, "is the matter of your concern for us. You have provided for us well enough. We have the house and we have a steady income. The Collick family has been most generous. You are a gentleman and have been quite open with me, yet you seem, forgive my forthrightness, you still appear disturbed."

Millie stopped abruptly, but Stephen only smiled his soft, unexpected smile.

"Millie, the Collick Estate has made a fortune on the back of your husband's genius. I, personally, am a rich man with no one to care for except myself. I have more money than I need and I know that much of what I have should be yours."

Millie's always rather stern face softened, partly with relief, partly from sympathy.

"I don't want any more money, Stephen. I am comfortably situated and it suits me to remain so. As for your wealth, you will probably marry and need all your money!"

His eyes flashed momentarily, almost too quickly to be noticed, before the smile returned.

"No, there is no likelihood of that, Millie. But it is my earnest wish to remain your friend, if you will permit me."

"Permit you? Of course I permit you. I am deeply honoured to be able to call you my friend, Stephen."

After some more tea, they left the hotel. For the return journey, Millie sat in the front passenger seat. To watch him work, she said.

Chapter Nine
1929 And the End of Innocence

In the end, the spring term passed without any of the fall-out from the Lacey party that Charlie had secretly feared. Although he had not heard a word from her since that night, Jennifer, on arrival at the Northern, greeted him as she greeted everyone, as an old friend. She made one of her usual gushing entrances, smiling, posing and chatting to everyone as if she had seen them all the previous day. The only thing missing was any indication of a special relationship with Charlie. That was now quite clearly a thing of the past.

Her stance came as a surprise to Charlie but suited him well. It was a relief. Forced by the events of the Highgate party to examine carefully both his own and other people's recent behaviour, he had come to certain conclusions. One of these was that he would no longer be Jennifer's puppy. He intended to withdraw from the Amateur Dramatic Society, the Orchestral Society and the Operatic Society.

His plans were thwarted to a degree by Bobby, who persuaded him to fill a gap in the chorus of *The Gondoliers* in the Operatic Society's spring production. They needed more chaps as "g-gondoliers," he said, and an imposing presence such as Charlie's would be an ideal addition. Bobby was sure Charlie loved being in the midst of all the activity of the production, no matter that he couldn't sing and didn't like acting. He would fill the space and look good

Charlie just shrugged, but went along with the idea willingly enough. He told himself that he had to do it for Bobby.

Always intelligent and quick witted, Charlie was seen at first by his new acquaintances as a quiet chap who only spoke when he had something to contribute to the conversation. Soon, though, he found himself drawn into the regular discussions at The Victoria Tavern or The George, just down the road. These could be triggered by a lecture at the Northern, news on the wireless or an article in a newspaper or magazine.

Whenever Charlie spoke, his words were listened to carefully. He had become known as a thinking man. The label was first applied by Bobby one Friday evening at the Victoria Tavern, after Alec Chapman had been expounding long-windedly a theory of his father's on how to end the evil of the trade unions. In a few sharply expressed sentences, Charlie had ripped the argument to shreds, to the uproarious delight of all present, except Alec.

The decision to join the chorus, however, fitted with Charlie's growing image of himself as a thinking man, no longer an adolescent. He appreciated the message of the Principal's initial address in the Great Hall, that 'the Polytechnic represented a changing world'. In Charlie's opinion, the Northern Polytechnic Institute was a highly significant establishment for the people of London. It was a modern institution, a sort of hybrid: a technical university for people of all classes.

It acknowledged the huge difference in lifestyle between the various groups of students studying at any one time. On the ground floor, for instance, the workshops were full of local teenagers, the apprentices and trainee craftspeople who would be the country's future tradesmen and factory foremen. But, up on the second floor, he and his fellow students were very much the white collared leaders of the future. They were the middle classes who would become the merchants of commerce and the managers of industry.

Yet, he marvelled, in the recreational areas, the non-academic areas, all were equal. All were encouraged to engage in the social activities of the Northern. People could do whatever interested them without fear of being made to feel uncomfortable. This modern, progressive attitude met with the full approval of Charlie Stoker, the thinker.

And so the year progressed for the fast maturing eighteen-year-old, a year in which the young man began to fulfil his parents' dream. He worked hard at the degree course, his father's course, while at the same time bathing in the joys of a student's life. Untouched by the bleak political and economic atmosphere that pervaded the country and most of the developed world, Charlie was enjoying life. It was by far the happiest and most exciting year of his life up to that time.

This feeling was enhanced, as the year progressed, by his awareness of a change in his mother's general bearing. For the first time in many years, she appeared contented. She was smiling and not weighed down by anxiety. She had started going out socially, although with whom or to where, she had not yet enlightened him.

Once the academic year ended, however, Millie did broach the subject. She asked him to consider foregoing a day of cycling or whatever else he was doing, and to remain at home one Sunday afternoon to enjoy tea with his mother and a guest. It was a request to which Charlie acceded with delight. Never, since his father's death, had any guest other than old Fr. Peter been invited to the house for tea.

"Yeah, happy to, but who's the guest?" he queried.

"Mr Stephen Collick. You remember him from the memorial service, perhaps?"

"I remember the Collicks, Dad's old bosses, weren't they? There was the old general in uniform and the tall chap that you went off to talk with."

"Yes. The tall gentleman was the Hon. Stephen Collick. He deals with all the business affairs of the Collick Estate. He has always been the link between them and our family."

"And is this tea a business affair?"

"No, Charlie, this is strictly a social visit. I want you to meet him and talk to him. Stephen is a kind gentleman who has expressed a strong desire to become a friend of the family. He was very close to your father before France, and it is only recently that, er…" She hesitated, "Perhaps, I should say, circumstances have only recently permitted a reconnection. I think you will like him."

Charlie shrugged.

"Yeah, okay."

After a pause, he added, "Are you getting especially friendly with him, then?"

Millie gave a little sigh.

"No, Charlie, not in that way. Your father and you have been, are, and will ever be the only men in my life. Nothing can alter that. Stephen Collick wishes simply to become a family friend, and I would like that, too."

* * *

Having allowed public access to the gardens since 1925, Lord Iveagh, on his death in 1927, bequeathed Kenwood House to the nation. This, his stately home on the northern edge of Hampstead Heath, complete with its magnificent collection of works of art, its landscaped gardens and its wild fringe of natural beauty that blended into the heath itself, was formally opened to the public the following year.

In 1929, Henry Whitworth decided Kenwood would be the perfect venue for the camera club's summer outing. So it was that Charlie parked his bicycle outside the gates just before ten o'clock on a Saturday morning in August. With his small knap-sack hanging from his left shoulder, he joined about a dozen or more members already gathered in small groups by the front entrance.

Everyone carried a bag or basket with a packed lunch, plus a Brownie camera or something of similar specification, and an unused roll of film. Jennifer Lacey was holding forth to one group, cigarette holder in hand, and she waved to him as he approached. He waved back but walked over to chat with Walter Hadkin, standing alone on the far side of the gate, studying the notice board. The two had become quite well acquainted during the year. Charlie respected the intelligence and knowledge of the timid photographer's assistant with the flappy ears, whom he was finding to be an invaluable source of tips on camerawork.

Walter thought that Charlie would enjoy the tour of the house. He himself had been lucky enough to visit a couple of times earlier in the year with his boss, who was sometimes commissioned to take photos there. The library was particularly beautiful, as were all the paintings, of course. Walter had studied art and eagerly transmitted his excitement about the Iveagh collection to his friend. There was a superb Rembrandt self-portrait, and a Vermeer, as well as paintings by Gainsborough, Turner and Reynolds. He'd tell him more about them as they went round, he promised.

Their conversation was interrupted by the arrival of Mr Whitworth, who nervously called everybody together and explained the plan for the day in his usual uncertain manner.

"It's a fine summer's day, isn't it? But, ah, before going off into the gardens to enjoy the, ah, weather, we are going to be treated to a guided tour of the house, as, ah, you know, of course, ah, and of the magnificent art collection that makes up the Iveagh Bequest. Once the house visit has been completed, ah, as a group, you will be free to, ah, wander all over the estate, and to, ah, enjoy a picnic lunch and to take your pictures."

The only obligation upon every member, he reminded them, was to take a photograph to be entered into the summer outing competition. This was a special competition designed to test imagination. They had all been asked to bring a small camera and a roll of film. They could use only the one roll of film, and the used rolls must be passed to Mr Whitworth, marked with the photographer's name, before the members left the estate between four-thirty and five o'clock in the afternoon. The films would all be developed in the club darkroom, and at the club meeting on the following Wednesday each member would select his own competition entry from his roll's printed results.

It was past midday by the time the house tour was completed, and they dispersed into groups to take lunch and photos. Charlie had been walking with Jennifer as they came to the end of the tour. Although no special relationship any longer existed between them, he still found her to be good company. He enjoyed intelligent conversation, and Jennifer was without doubt intelligent. She was also a sunny presence in any crowd. Like Walter, she had been here before, and was pleased to show off her knowledge of the art collection as they went around. Between the two of them, they force-fed Charlie with knowledge of fine art, a subject in which he had little interest; but he took it all in good part, with a few shrugs and the odd question.

The members formed into their lunch groups, and Charlie and Jennifer were joined by Walter Hadkin and then by Jennifer's friend Margret Mabey, who, it seemed to Charlie, materialised out of thin air. He had not seen her at all since his arrival at Kenwood, but suddenly the two girls were chatting as if they had been together all morning. They were joined by two other members, Kay Cheriton and Violet Perry, also students at the Northern, and the six found a secluded area under the trees beyond the formal gardens in which to enjoy a leisurely lunch in the warm, still air.

Jennifer produced a large white sheet that they spread over the ground. Then they all opened their lunch boxes and baskets, and pooled the contents. In addition to the spread of food, Jennifer produced a flask filled with Irish whisky and lemonade, plus a bottle of water. Margret and Kay had each brought a bottle of red wine, and the other three members, beer or soft drinks. Altogether, it made for a grand lunch party.

Conversation, at first subdued and polite, gradually became louder and less restrained as the alcohol disappeared. Topics ranged widely, from the death earlier that week of Serge Diaghilev to the merits of different cigarette brands; and from the marriage of the handsome young film stars Douglas Fairbanks Jnr. and Joan Crawford to the disastrous state of world affairs and the state of the country.

Of course, politics was never far away from conversations among the students of the Northern, but Charlie was fascinated to hear, after a few mixed drinks, a fierce outburst from, of all people, Walter. It was outrageous, he protested, that one of the first actions of the new Labour government was to increase the price of milk. There was no work for ordinary people and they put up the price of milk! And this from a socialist government, the party of the people!

Unexpected and forceful as this utterance was from the quiet photographer, all were unprepared for what followed. Jennifer tore into poor Walter with what Charlie now recognised as a typically uncontrolled tirade. She ranted that this could hardly be blamed on the new government. After all, they had only inherited the current state of affairs. It was simply down to economics, as any fool should know! Businesses everywhere were facing financial pressures. The country was still trying to pay for the cost of the Great War, for goodness sake!

Her voice became shriller and her colour more heightened as her arguments gathered pace. Retail prices had been falling for ten years but raw materials had to be imported from overseas, and were costing more money. There were huge and ever-growing numbers of unemployed throughout the midlands and the north unable to contribute to the public purse and needing money to live on, but the country still had to pay its way. If they couldn't raise it in income tax they had to find it from somewhere else!

The ferocity of the salvo completely silenced a white-faced Walter and everyone else for a time. The photographer retreated in the face of superior forces and nervously sought the last of the burgundy. Kay and Violet whispered to each other behind their hands, and Charlie, eyes twinkling, shrugged sympathetically at Walter. Margret carefully lit a cigarette and blew a smoke ring before observing airily for all to hear:

"I see your father's been sounding off again, Jennifer."

"Oh-h, Margret!!!"

Jennifer slapped her arms against her thighs in shamed exasperation and flounced off to find the ladies cloakroom. The others slowly recovered from the Lacey storm and resumed less passionate conversations. When Jennifer returned ten minutes later, she was her smiling, chatty self again. She lit a Craven 'A', and began a conversation with Kay.

Eventually, it was Margret Mabey who brought the group's attention back to the afternoon ahead. Were they going to move as a group or break up?

Walter made it clear at once that he preferred to work alone and would just like to wander off on his own. Jennifer thought that was a good idea, she would do the same. It would be easier to concentrate, she thought. Kay and Violet opted to go together.

"Well, that leaves only us, Big Boy," said Margret to Charlie. She spoke casually but her deep-set brown eyes were looking at him meaningfully. "Shall we hunt as a pair?"

Charlie had not considered this situation. He had expected to have Walter's company all day and to be led by him. The girls, as girls always did, would go off in pairs. But suddenly a much more interesting afternoon was in prospect. Margret Mabey!

Margret was something of an enigma to Charlie. When they had been first introduced, at the club Xmas party, he had thought her to be a bit of a blue stocking. Then, at Jennifer's party he could not remember seeing her to speak to at all; but his impression today was of quite a different person.

She was tall for a girl, and thin. She was wearing a light brown day dress with a fashionable dropped waist. It particularly suited her long body and her pale, angular features. Her face was not beautiful like Jennifer's, but there was something about Margret. She had a maturity and a quiet self-confidence that indicated a knowledge of life beyond her years. To a healthy eighteen-year-old student who had partaken of alcohol on a summer's day, she was, to put it bluntly, damned attractive. Charlie lifted his knapsack onto his lap to cover his embarrassment.

"Yes, why not?" he replied enthusiastically.

Everyone put the debris from their meal back into their baskets and knapsacks, and they rolled up the big sheet. The area restored as nearly as possible to its former state, they set off on their various paths.

Gentleman Charlie attempted to carry Margret's basket for her, but she disdainfully pulled it out of his reach.

"Well, which way we should go from here, Margret?" he asked a little tentatively. "You know, don't you, that I have neither attended a camera club summer trip nor visited Kenwood before today? I'm a bit of an innocent about this sort of thing."

She turned her knowing smile onto him. "You're a bit of an innocent about a lot of things, Big Boy. I think we'll have to do something about you."

Charlie grinned. "Oh yes? Such as?"

"Ha! You'll soon see. Let's go."

She set off at once, striding not in the direction of the formal gardens to which all the others had headed, but diagonally across the open grass towards the far side of the house. Charlie dutifully strode alongside in the hot afternoon sun.

"You see," she said confidentially, lowering her voice and slowing their pace, "I know this place rather well. I came here a few times when Lord Iveagh was still alive. Our two families have always been friends since Great Uncle Rupert was at university with Edward Guinness, as he then was, more than sixty years ago. Lady Dorothy, Lord Iveagh's granddaughter, is my age—about three months older, I think. We got on well together when I spent a weekend with her here five years ago. There's a walled garden to the left of the house that is separate from the main park and is very unspoiled. It stretches back quite a long way but people simply don't know it is there. We used to wander around the woods in there. It is quite beautiful. We called it our secret hideaway."

"Wow! No wonder you're grinning. I didn't realise you were so well connected. Lord Iveagh was one of the richest men in the country, wasn't he? I'm not sure I can afford to be in your company, Margret."

Charlie made the comment lightly, but did not feel at ease inside.

"Oh, Big Boy, where have you been all your life? He was only an Irish brewer, you know. Yes, he came from a good family, but so did we. The only difference was that they were astute businessmen and my lot were just farmers. They made lots of boodle and we didn't. My father studied law and got lucky, he got out; but my uncles are still ploughing for pennies."

Charlie shrugged and said nothing. There wasn't much he could say. Suddenly, he was moving in a different world.

They went through a small gate hidden behind some trees near the house, and it was as if they had been transported like Alice in Wonderland. The only sounds were the sounds of nature undisturbed, the twittering of birds and the rustling of leaves.

"Well, I'll be blowed!" exclaimed Charlie. He shook his head in wonderment and turned to Margret, laughing beside him. "I really didn't expect anything like this."

"No, I don't expect you did, my handsome. Come, I'll show you the hideaway."

About fifty yards ahead, a dense copse lay behind a ten-foot-high hedge of elderberry, hawthorn and lilac. Margret, followed closely by Charlie, threaded her way through a clump of bushes and into a grassy space no more than five yards square. An old wooden bench stood on one side. She sat down on the bench, put her basket on the ground and held out a hand for Charlie to join her. He did so, with a gush of expelled air and a grunt.

"Well, shiver my timbers! As my grandfather would have said."

Margret smiled, the smile of a cat that has just got the cream. "I thought you'd be surprised," she said.

They sat for some time, enjoying the stillness of the air and the privacy of their hideaway. In a state of reverie, Charlie thought about her voice. It was deep and melodious. It reminded him of someone else, but he could not think whom.

"You know," he said slowly, "I see you as a different person today. You look so happy and at peace. I've never seen you like that before."

She laughed and placed her hand gently on his thigh. "I think you have, Charlie, my Big Boy, you surely have."

"No, I haven't Margret, honestly. To tell the truth, I thought you were a bit of a blue stocking, but today I can see the real you and—." He stopped, suddenly embarrassed. "Would you like a cigarette?"

"Not just now, Big Boy, maybe later." Her hand was still resting on his thigh, and she pressed downwards gently as she spoke, then raised her hand in affirmation of her words.

Charlie rather hurriedly placed his knapsack on his knee again.

Margret said, in a deliberately sultry tone: "Would you think I were a blue stocking if I were wearing a cream trouser suit, Charlie?"

There was silence for a second or two before the penny dropped. Realisation struck him like a thunderbolt.

"The silken angel! Oh, my G—d! It was you! You were the angel!"

Margret burst into laughter. "Angel? I'm no angel! Oh, Big Boy, you should see your face! Who did you think it was, for goodness sake?"

"But, but I had no idea, Margret, honestly. I was so drunk that night, and my memory of what happened after I left Mr Lacey is all vague and confused. All I remember is a beautiful vision in silk—you! Putting me to bed and then vanishing."

"Vanishing? Are you sure that is all you remember?"

"I remember you suddenly appearing and supporting me on the stairs, and…"

She drew up her skirt to display her long, slender legs, then placed her hand on his thigh again, this time not allowing it to remain static. She moved it slowly up and down. "Nothing else? Can't you remember what else we did?"

Now, the smile was wicked. She moved so that her upper body was pressing against him. Charlie felt it like an electric shock. He put his hand on hers to temper the affect she was having upon him, but the result was the opposite. Her smell and her touch were overwhelming. His arms reached out, and the knapsack tumbled to the ground.

* * *

On the Sunday afternoon of the weekend following the camera club outing, a gleaming Lanchester motorcar sat outside the house in Amhurst Road. Inside, Florrie Brown, specially recruited on a Sunday and in a new white apron, served afternoon tea in the upstairs sitting room for Charlie, his mother and their gentleman guest, the Hon. Stephen Collick.

The occasion, although informal, was significant for each of them. For Stephen, it represented further success in his efforts to befriend the family of Charles Stoker. For Millie, it was a confirmation that a normal life was possible for her after *that* day; and for Charlie, it was a social engagement, his first experience of what he supposed was, in most homes, a traditionally normal part of life.

At first meeting, Stephen Collick always appeared to be a rather diffident, nervous person, but once comfortable with his environment he became an easy and accomplished conversationalist. Indeed, he was a well-travelled and knowledgeable man, with a wide experience of life, both in war and peace. He brought wide smiles to the faces of Millie and Charlie with reminiscences of some of his business trips. They both listened with rapt attention.

The tone of conversation changed significantly when Millie was called downstairs by Florrie, leaving the two men alone. Collick asked Charlie about his studies and his plans for the future.

"I'm doing physics and maths at the Northern, but I haven't decided what I'll do afterwards. My father wanted me to get the same degree as him, and my mother has sort of kept me to it."

Charlie shrugged and smiled.

"It's alright, though, I s'pose I can do anything afterwards, but at least I'll have got a degree. As for what, I really don't know. I want to build the shoe business, but my mother's not sure that's the way to go."

Stephen Collick nodded his approval.

"Yes, a sound education is invariably a firm step to a successful career. Your mother is an extremely sensible woman. Indeed, both your parents have been." He paused, studying Charlie. "You know, you are awfully like your father, both in build and appearance. You have the same blond hair and blue eyes—and you have his smile."

Charlie shrugged.

"How well did you actually know him? Mum said that you had worked together but I don't remember you ever visiting here."

"No, I suppose not. You would have been very young."

The diffidence and nervousness had resurfaced. Then Stephen Collick leaned forward, placing his hands upon his knees. He spoke very purposefully:

"Charlie, your father and I began our careers at Clerkenwell in the same year. We were both fresh from university, and I was very much drawn to him from the first day I knew him. We became good colleagues and good friends. He was a remarkable man, most remarkable. He had a calmness, a composed self-assurance at all times, and the most disarming smile I have ever known. He was also a brilliant engineer and inventor. The more deeply he became involved in the business, the more innovative became his ideas."

"I-I," he stuttered over the pronoun and hesitated before continuing, "I admired your father immensely, from the early days until the day he died, regardless of the distance that he placed between us. When I heard about the riot and its disastrous consequence, I made a vow to provide for your family for as long as I lived."

Charlie failed to greet these words with his usual shrug and grin, considering them carefully for some time. They made no sense to him. Eventually, he simply voiced his thoughts:

"I don't understand why you would do that. If you were such good friends and colleagues with my dad, why did we never meet you? Why have I never heard about you all my life? I'm eighteen years old!"

"Charlie, how dare you!" Millie, re-entering the room, heard her son's words.

"No, Millie, please!"

Stephen Collick held up his hand commandingly, and Millie halted by the door. Stephen suggested she sit, and she did so, meek and wordless. He immediately became his diffident self again.

"Charlie is absolutely right to express his confusion, Millie. Am I correct in assuming he knows nothing of the past or of our previous conversations?"

"No. I mean, yes, you are correct, Stephen. Charles never spoke of his war service after he came home, and he always strongly discouraged any questions on the subject. I have simply continued in the same manner. It seemed the best way."

Collick nodded. "Yes, I imagine so, quite so."

He paused, then addressed Millie again, his tone once more deferential.

"Millie, you have suffered enough pain all these years. Would it not perhaps be wise, now, now that you are finding some peace, for your son to understand the full picture?"

Millie wrung her hands.

"You are right of course, Stephen. It was just that, after eleven years of silence..." She raised her hands in surrender. Stephen turned to Charlie.

"As I mentioned just now, your father and I were good friends and colleagues, way back before 1910, when you were born. Indeed, I met you on two or three occasions when you were very small, before 1914. Once the war came, however, everything changed. We lost touch."

"At the service of remembrance that you attended for your father, respect was shown for him as an officer, a major in the Royal Flying Corps; a flier who had lost a limb fighting for his country, and whose life had been cut short by that catastrophe in May 1926." He paused. "But that was by no means the whole story, Charlie."

Stephen Collick then related the conversation he had shared with Millie a couple of months earlier. He missed out nothing, emphasising how much he and his family owed to Charles. He ended by passionately re-iterating his conviction that Charles Stoker had been denied the recognition and reward due to him as a war hero, one worthy of the highest honours.

Charlie sat still, his face like stone. After a long silence, he shrugged.

"So what?" he said. "He was still a cripple. The cripple built this shoe business on one leg. And he was still a hero—my father's always been a hero to me. What difference would another medal make?"

The teenager glowered challengingly at the baron's son. Stephen glanced fleetingly at Millie, whose index finger was in front of her mouth. He acknowledged with the faintest movement.

"You are right, Charlie," he said. "He was a hero to all three of us. I am afraid I am no hero, but would you please allow me to be a friend?"

The glower faded. Charlie shrugged, the hint of a smile forming around his blue eyes. "Okay," he said.

Chapter Ten
Margret

Margret Cavendish Mabey was born in January, 1910, on the family estate by the river Barrow in County Carlow in the south-east of Ireland. When she was just a month old, however, her father, Herbert Mabey, became a partner in a legal practice in Enfield in Middlesex.

The position had arisen because his uncle, Rupert Cavendish, the founder of the partnership, became seriously ill. Rupert, aged sixty-four, was the brother of Herbert's mother and a bachelor, who, although from a catholic family, had earned his degree at Trinity College, Dublin. His nephew had followed him there thirty years later, and it had always been Rupert's intention that the young man should take his place upon his retirement.

By the time the sick Rupert died, three years later in 1913, Herbert Mabey had settled with his wife and three children in a large house set in two acres of land just off Clay Hill, to the northwest of Enfield Town. It was an ideal residence for someone intending to become a figure in the community. Certainly, the practice was already comfortably the larger and more well-established of the two in the High Street. Rupert Cavendish, with his partner, Laurence Brigham, had built a successful business dealing principally with the everyday legal affairs of the local middle classes: land and property contracts, wills and investments; and avoiding involvement in criminal law beyond the petty offences that occasionally involved their clients and were dealt with by the local magistrates.

Herbert, though, had grander ideas. Young and aggressive, he intended to broaden their horizons, to inject new life into the business. His plans were soon halted by the declaration of war in 1914. He answered the call to serve in The Duke of Cambridge's Own, the Middlesex Regiment.

He served the full four years with the 1/7th Battalion, Middlesex Regiment, and whatever his experiences in the war—he always avoided talking about them to his family—he returned in 1918 apparently unscathed, and promptly set about shaking up the legal practice. His dynamism and acuity enabled the practice to grow over the next decade to become the largest in Middlesex north of Tottenham.

Herbert Mabey planned for his children to follow him into the practice, and Harry, Margret's brother and three years her elder, was educated at Harrow and Trinity College, Oxford before taking his place as a junior solicitor in the practice in 1928.

Margret, however, had other ideas. She had always been of a rebellious nature and something of a loner who had made no real friends at the private school she attended as a day pupil. Her annual reports showed her to be a brilliant but difficult pupil, not that this concerned her at all. She enjoyed studying, particularly mathematics and literature, she played hockey and she painted for pleasure. She also loved riding and kept her own pony at the stables along the road.

What she did not do, however, was to make friends easily. Margret did not suffer fools gladly; indeed, she did not suffer them at all. As a child, her definition of a fool would be anyone who disagreed with her, but as she grew older it was moderated to mean anyone whom she considered to be lacking in intellect.

She had a stormy and generally antagonistic relationship with both of her brothers from an early age. She regarded them both as stupid. From the age of five, she had had but one close friend. Introduced to Jennifer Lacey, the daughter of one of her father's fellow officers, and several months younger than she, the two had soon become inseparable. Jennifer, a beautiful, quick-witted child, was immediately overawed by the precocious Margaret and remained so throughout her childhood. Wherever Margret led, Jennifer followed, and the arrangement seemed to suit them both.

Over time, Jennifer gradually came to echo Margret's words and to adopt her attitudes. While this was of no account in the loftily cold atmosphere of the Mabey house, where Margret was accepted as a rebellious second child and her antics were to a large extent ignored, it was unacceptable to Mrs Lacey in the Highgate household. There, a warm, welcoming atmosphere pervaded at all times, and Jennifer, the eldest of four children, was made to conform to the family's standards of behaviour.

Thus, Margret's influence was countered to a great extent. By the time Jennifer reached adolescence it showed only in occasional inexplicable outbursts of intolerant temper, often prompted by the consumption of alcohol, a plentiful commodity in the Lacey home after 1918. The friendship between the two girls, though, remained firm.

When the time came for decisions about Margret's future, she was called into her father's study, where his insistence that she study for a law degree was bluntly rejected. She told him that she had no intention of becoming a chattel in the family firm. She had decided instead that her future role was to be an academic one, for which she intended to study mathematics. After much screaming and shouting between father and daughter, Margret emerged victorious. In September 1928, she was enrolled at the London School of Economics to study mathematics and economics.

In most respects, Margret Mabey's first year at university went according to plan. She had the privacy of her own room on the ground floor in the small female hall of residence; her tutors recognised at once her exceptional qualities, and her fellow students tended to fall into two categories: the few who were able to interact with her on her own intellectual level, whom she treated as equals; and the rest whom she largely ignored.

The only thing that did not work out was her hope that Jennifer would join her at the university. She was briefly irritated with her friend for not rebelling as she had, and for following timidly into her father's profession; but then she acknowledged to herself that Jennifer was well-suited to the pharmaceutical career and the chemist's shop.

Jennifer Lacey's coy smile and her tendency to adopt attentive poses caught people's attention. It had won her instant friends at school and again at college, and it endeared her to the customers in the chemist's shop. It did not, however, encourage long-term relationships. Once people grew accustomed to her instant brightness and her desperate need to impress, they often tired of her. The truth was that there was little depth to Jennifer. She was stunning to look at, bright and quick-witted, but essentially shallow of intellect.

If Margret had thought this of any other person in the world, she would have discarded that person long ago. But her relationship with Jennifer was different. In so far as it was possible for Margaret Mabey to love anyone, she had grown to love Jennifer. From their first meeting, when she was just five, the four-year-old Jennifer had shown her nothing but love, trust and friendship, all sentiments foreign to the Mabey household.

No matter how badly she treated her younger friend, and at times she had been viciously cruel, that love had never wavered. There had been many tears, many screams and many scratches over the years, but always there would be forgiveness and understanding from Jennifer. Never was there the numbing coldness she experienced from her own family.

Indeed, Jennifer was probably the only person in the world she did love. Most certainly, she held no such feeling for her own kin. She had concluded, years earlier, that the Mabeys were a clan of mean, impoverished Irish farmers who would stop at nothing in their efforts to regain their lost wealth and standing. They would trample upon anyone and anything.

Her father, cunning cold fish that he was, was no exception in character—he was a nasty bully of a man, but he had found a different route. He had deserted the family home at the first opportunity, to enjoy an easier life practising law in England, where he had seized the chance to become a big fish in his small suburban pond.

His wife, her mother Mairead, was viewed by her daughter as a despicable mouse who was content to do his bidding in all matters. She bore his children, maintained the home to his desired standards, and never questioned his authority, his judgement or his attitudes.

Their three children, when young, had been left in the charge of a nursemaid and taught not to bother their parents. Thereafter, the boys had been packed off to school. For Margret, however, a tutor was brought in until she was old enough to attend a suitable day school.

The reason for this was expressed succinctly by her father. They were boys and she, unfortunately, was a girl.

* * *

After the camera club outing, Charlie and Margret met on several occasions throughout the autumn of 1929. Charlie was enjoying a full and exciting life at the Northern. He now had a full schedule of lectures, and was maintaining his cycling and swimming activities; but what developed with Margret was something apart.

Unusually tall for a woman, the thin, severe-looking solicitor's daughter was like no other person Charlie had come across in his nearly nineteen years. She found his physical build attractive, and liked that he appeared impervious to her sharp, at times acerbic, manner. As for him, Charlie appreciated her wit and intelligence, to say nothing of her sexual expertise.

From the first, Margret set about educating him in ways to satisfy them both, and he proved a willing and able learner. She sneaked him into her room in the hall of residence, where they engaged in extensive practice sessions. One evening, he asked her where she had learned to be so proficient in the art of lovemaking.

"My brother Harry started using me to practice on when I was about nine," she replied nonchalantly. "He forced me to do things, but eventually stopped when I bit him. I nearly bit it off. Then, when I was about thirteen, the boy who looked after the horses at the stables across the road kept gazing at me as if he wanted to romp a bit but didn't dare, so one day I let him and found I liked it. So we did it again."

Everything that Margret did and said was to some degree shocking to Charlie, but he rarely allowed it to show. The shrug and the grin were his defensive barriers. He never wasted words. It was enough that they both enjoyed their sexual encounters. Both relished the secrecy of their arrangement.

When she suggested that he visit her at the family home in Enfield on the last day of October, a Saturday, Charlie happily shrugged his acceptance of the idea. Her parents were away for the weekend, she explained. Although her family were ghastly, she loved the house, the garden and her horse. There was a tennis court and they could play tennis if he chose to.

Having apologised to Bobby for missing their Saturday swim, Charlie cycled to Enfield for his first visit to the house at Clay Hill. On a fine day, after a week of bad weather, he arrived at the imposing residence just after ten o'clock to be welcomed by an odd-looking little woman in black, wearing a white apron, who 'was pleashed to lead him to Mish Margret in the garden shitting room'.

Margret was sitting on a sofa in the small sitting room, by the French window that opened to a terrace with steps to a large lawn. She did not get up. "Thank you, Betsy. I shall manage from here, Betsy. Off you go to see your mother. You'll be pleased to have a weekend off."

"Yesh, mish, thank you, mish,"

The little woman curtsied and disappeared. Margret, looking fresh in a white tennis skirt and blouse, reached out, ushering Charlie to her side.

"Come here, Big Boy. That was Betsy, she's a bit soft in the head, but she does her job well enough."

Charlie sat down with a shrug.

The day went well, and they enjoyed the pleasant late October weather together. They explored the garden, which stretched through some well-placed trees to the small river that ran around the perimeter. Then they played tennis on the family's grass court, where the willing young man was well trounced.

Later, after a cold lunch, pre-prepared by Betsy and laid out for them on the dining room table complete with a bottle of red wine, they spent the afternoon exploring each other on the large bed in her room.

Tea was then taken on the terrace, Margret producing a platter of scones and cream cakes that Charlie did his best to devour, dressed now in a Mabey dressing gown, and nonchalantly smoking a cigarette as he admired the view of Margret's long legs. Margret wore a light jacket loosely over a peach negligee that displayed those legs to distraction.

Suddenly, she pointed upwards and shouted.

"Look!"

Following her outstretched arm, he looked up sharply. Travelling slowly, and at little more than 1000ft. above the ground, was a massive airship. It was a stunning sight, a long, silver flying fish moving in stately manner from south to north across the sky, below the wispy clouds. They both stared at the huge machine for some time before Margret broke the silence.

"It must feel extremely liberating to be able to fly off into the clouds like that."

Charlie, still staring upwards, was slow to reply.

"Yeah," he said, "I suppose that's how my dad felt when he first went up."

"Your dad? Oh yes, you said your father flew in the war, didn't you? That must have been fun."

"Yeah."

"I think you also said your father was invalided in 1917. Was that to do with his flying?"

"Yes. He was shot down, he crashed."

"Oh, merde! I'm sorry, Big Boy. Was I being tactless?"

Charlie exhaled a cloud of smoke with a shrug.

"No more than usual," he said.

"Brute!"

Charlie nodded upwards, bringing the conversation back to the airship. "That's the R101 on its way back to Cardington, I read about it yesterday in the Chronicle."

"It's enormous, isn't it? It looks a mile long!"

"Yeah, it's big alright. Actually, it's about two hundred and fifty yards long."

"Gracious! Really?" Margret stared for a few more moments, then asked, "Would you like to fly, like your father, Charlie?"

Charlie concentrated on his cigarette.

"No," he said.

Margret did not press him further.

* * *

For Millie Stoker, life was at last comfortable. She was even becoming quite socially active. Her nineteen-year-old son also seemed to be enjoying life, and living it to the fullest. He was still enjoying his weekly swim with his friend Bobby, and cycling, although Bobby rarely cycled now, preferring to spend his time with his motorcycle and with his girlfriend, Daphne.

At the end of November, Charlie persuaded his mother to accompany him to a concert at the Northern, the first time they had shared an outing, other than to the church, for more than four years. He introduced her to Bobby and Daphne, and to Jennifer.

She had previously met Bobby, briefly, at Amhurst Road one day when the boys had been cycling; but on that occasion, the poor chap had not been able to get past the first few minutes' stammering. It was a pleasant surprise, therefore, to meet the real, relaxed Bobby Bruce. Daphne, she thought was a sweet girl, and Jennifer was undoubtedly a beauty.

Afterwards, they all went across to the Victoria Tavern for a nightcap, where Millie, embarrassed to be in such an establishment, sipped a lemonade. She spoke very little, but thoroughly enjoyed being with the young people. She also gained a good idea of the humour of the younger generation. Jennifer had introduced the subject of the Nobel prizes announced that week.

"The prize for literature has gone to the German author, Thomas Mann," she announced to the table, flamboyantly holding her cigarette in its holder, her arm outstretched. "Have any of you read his work?"

"No, 'fraid not," replied Daphne. "I did literature at school but it was all English writers. I've not read much foreign stuff. Is he good?"

"God help me! He's magnificent!" She turned to Charlie.

"Haven't you heard of *Buddenbrooks*? It's a huge work, a magnificent work. Mann is one of the most powerful voices in modern literature."

"Oh? No, sorry, I'm not well up on it. I've studied sciences more than the arts. There are some classics on the bookshelf at home but I've not read many, apart from Dickens. Oh, and Swift; and Shakespeare, but I liked the Dickens books."

"David Copperfield is my very favourite novel," interposed Daphne with awe in her voice.

"Yeah, I've read that," added Bobby in support, without a stutter.

"Dickens was a great storyteller, but Mann is a great thinker."

Jennifer declaimed, in an arch tone, words that smacked, to Charlie, of Margret Mabey.

"He writes in the most beautiful language but with a tortured soul. His work is always concerned with the pain of the existence of the creative artist. One can quite understand his award of the Nobel Prize."

"I heard that was why he had a large n-knocker on his d-door." stuttered Bobby with a wide grin, "H-he wanted to win the N-N-No-bell prize."

Jennifer said, "Oh, my God!" in a loud voice and slapped the table in irritation. Daphne burst into giggles. Charlie winced and grinned.

Watching Charlie with his friends, Millie detected a significant change in his bearing. He was still a quiet chap, but there was an air about him, a self-confidence that reminded her of his father. She felt very proud.

Margret was not present that night, but that was not surprising. She quite often did not bother to attend their social events. In fact, Charlie had not seen her since the day of their sighting of the R101, but he had been particularly busy for a few weeks and he supposed she had too.

Chapter Eleven
1930

The roaring twenties, decade of opportunity for so many and of poverty for so many more, ended with the great crash of the American stock market. The repercussions were felt worldwide. Great Britain, insulated to some extent by her colonial links, suffered less than the rest of Europe, but exports collapsed, unemployment rose dramatically to reach twenty percent, and depression took hold of the country.

Billy Walters regarded himself as one of the lucky ones. He had continued to run the shoe repair shop successfully and had re-established a solid customer base. His unassuming, co-operative nature was especially appreciated by those customers who often needed shoes repaired on Monday that could not be paid for until Friday, if at all.

By 1929, Billy had earned the complete trust of Millie Stoker. She was quite content to accept his judgement, whether on material costs or on the reliability of any debtors. Indeed, during October and November of 1929, business was so good that it was necessary to employ an assistant for a few weeks.

At the end of the year, Millie agreed to close the shop for a week between Christmas and the New Year, so that Billy could marry and enjoy a short honeymoon. His bride was no other than Sally Biskin, the quiet girl who had called for help for Charles on *that* day. They planned to stay at Billy's mother's house until they could save enough to afford their own home, and Millie showed her approval of the match by giving them a wedding gift of ten pounds to help pay the cost of setting up their marriage home.

* * *

And so began the thirties, with a bitter winter. On a cold Sunday afternoon in January, Charlie returned home from a cycling trip to find his mother awaiting him with a message from Margret.

"That's the girl you met on the camera club summer outing, isn't it?" inquired Millie, "The girl who lives at Enfield? She sounds a very well-spoken girl."

Charlie grinned. "Yeah, she is, Mum. She can be a bit odd, she's a bit of a rebel, but she's good company, and very bright."

"She asked if you can meet her at the usual place tomorrow."

Charlie shrugged.

"Yeah, OK. It means I may be late tomorrow."

"That's all right. You're a big boy now."

She headed to the kitchen.

The usual place was a coffee house in Clare Market popular with the students. It was situated directly across the road from the college residence. It was unusual for them to meet on a Monday evening, but it happened to be a free night for Charlie, so he was quite happy to cycle into the city and park his bike in the rack. He found Margret sitting at a table for two near the door.

She looked up as he entered, but without her usual self-confident, slightly scornful smile. Instead, she stared at him with a stone-grey face, features drawn and eyes narrowed. His nonchalant air faded to a look of concern.

"Margret, it's good to see you, but you look awful! What's amiss? I was expecting a call, you said you were going away and would call in the New Year. But you don't look well. Tell me, what's wrong?"

This was certainly not a typical Charlie greeting, but he had been quite thrown by the sight of her.

"Charlie, sit down, and shut up!"

She hissed the words at him without any change of expression.

Charlie's twinkle returned to his eyes. That was more like her. He shrugged and sat.

"I am not ill," she continued, "I am not suffering from consumption, I have not contracted pneumonia, nor have I suffered a heart attack."

Silence from Charlie. She took a deep breath, then went on:

"Big Boy, I am pregnant."

Charlie looked at her quizzically.

"Yes, pregnant."

Then, suddenly spitting words at him with eyes blazing, she hissed:

"I, Margret Mabey, am pregnant!"

The twinkle vanished.

"Pregnant?" he whispered. "What do you mean, pregnant? How can you be pregnant?"

"I am pregnant, you big oaf, because I am going to have a baby. I am going to have a baby because you impregnated me with your sperm. You fucked me into pregnancy."

Charlie stared, stunned. He lit a cigarette and inhaled deeply. He had never heard a woman use that language before, and the first ludicrous thought that occurred to him was that Margret was probably the only woman in the world who could say it without loss of dignity.

"But, but you said it was alright," he blustered, bursting a cloud of smoke into the air. "You have been doing it for years, you said. You would show me how to really do it, you said. And you did, Margret! And you kept telling me not to worry. You always knew what you were doing…"

Charlie sucked on the cigarette in an effort to calm himself. He needed to take a mature view of this. Keep a clear head like his mother. He drew a deep breath.

Margret maintained her glare for a few more seconds, then, quite suddenly, her body sagged, her head dropped into the cushion of her folded arms on the table and she began to shake with sobs.

At first, Charlie watched helplessly, then he rose and went to the counter to fetch a glass of water. He placed it on the table next to her and took his folded handkerchief from his jacket pocket. Pressing it into Margret's hand, he left his own hand resting gently on hers. In time, the sobs subsided and Margret used the handkerchief to dry the tears. She took some water. After a further long moment, during which she fought to regain control of her emotions, she spoke again, quietly and deliberately:

"Big Boy, we have made a botch of things." She hesitated. "Or, rather, I, cocksure, ever clever Margret, have made the most colossal botch of things."

"You probably haven't," said Charlie, "but let's talk about it calmly, Marg."

She smiled weakly at the affectionate shortening of her name, something that at any other time she would have objected to fiercely. Charlie continued:

"I don't know much about this sort of thing, but help me. Let's establish the facts. Firstly, how sure are you? Has the doctor confirmed it? Could it be a false alarm? I understand that can happen."

Charlie's need to better understand the matter brought a positive response from Margret. Establishing facts was what she was good at. The budding academic drew a breath and delivered a lecture:

"Very well, Charlie Stoker, listen and learn. Listen and make notes. All women experience a menstrual cycle. The menstrual cycle is typically 28 days long, but that can vary from person to person. For most it is a nuisance for a few days each month; for others it creates more difficulties. For all, though, there will be times, usually from about the ninth or tenth day until about the nineteenth day, when sexual intimacy may well lead to pregnancy."

"Outside these days the risk diminishes. It is most unlikely to occur before the sixth day or after the twenty-second day of a cycle. If menstruation fails to take place on time, it is probably because a woman is pregnant, but it can be for other health related reasons. If it does not appear by the end of the second month, pregnancy is a certainty."

"My own cycle has always been as regular as night and day. It causes me little trouble and is over in a day or two. For seven years, I have menstruated within a day of the date each month, except for the couple of times when I had a fever and was perhaps a few days early or late."

"Yes, and as you have learned well, I delight in copulation. I love the moments of ecstasy and the extraordinary feeling of power that goes with it. It is what I am, it's my wild Irish blood... But, and it is a big but, I assure you, Big Boy, I have always indulged my desires on safe days. I have never deviated from this rule; or, rather, I had not deviated until our day together at Clay Hill."

"That was my sixth day. I was aware of a minimal risk, but I took the risk because it was you, damn you. There is something about you that makes a girl lose her head. Since then, I have failed to menstruate for two complete cycles. That means—and you can be assured that it does mean—I am with child, *your* child."

For the briefest moment the incongruous hint of a smile appeared in Charlie's eyes, but he refrained from comment. Margret drank some water. Her colour was better now, and her face less strained. Charlie said,

"We need some air. Have you eaten anything? How about a pint and a pie at the Old Wheatsheaf?"

Margret stood up without answering. She slipped on the fur-trimmed beige woollen coat that had been folded on her lap and walked through the door that Charlie was holding open. She took his arm and they walked in silence the short distance to the pub.

The Wheatsheaf was a comfortable public house, its unoccupied saloon bar warmed by a well-set fire. Charlie ordered two steak pies, a pint of pale ale for Margret and a brown ale for himself. He carried the drinks to the table, but waited until their hot pies had been served before he spoke again. Then he said, very precisely, in a low voice:

"Please tell me, just to be clear, does what you have said mean that you have reached the point, now, at which nothing can prevent the birth?"

"Birth is never certain, but short of a catastrophe or a deliberate act of destruction the child will be born early in the month of August."

"Have you told your mother?"

"Don't be stupid! She may well have guessed, though, by my behaviour during the last week or two before term. There are signs that women recognise."

"Alright. Then let's be logical about it. I don't know how I am supposed to feel, how I am supposed to react to this, but you know I will do the right thing by you. I shall not run away nor desert you, Marg, but it has to be a matter of what you want."

"My name is Margret!"

Charlie grinned. Margret glared at him, then softened the look and said:

"What I want, Big Boy, is for it all to go away. I want to get my degree and to teach mathematics."

The anger returned to her eyes.

"I want not to be pregnant. I want the world to go back to where it was three months ago. I want to be able to romp with you when I feel like it."

Her voice became sharper and louder.

"I want to be free of all this. I want to be able to live again. Oh my God, I want to die!"

Charlie moved around the table and took her in his arms as the tears flowed once more. He held her until she settled again, then returned to his seat and lit two cigarettes. He passed one to Margret. They sat, looking at each other.

"It's alright, old girl," Charlie said reassuringly, "I can see the path through this."

Margret looked up sharply at the firm tone of his voice. It was not what she expected. This was not the big, soft, quiet chap she was used to leading by the nose. This was a new Big Boy. This was a man in control of the situation, in control of her. Remarkably, she felt good about it.

Charlie asked: "How long can you continue your studies before you need to stop?"

"Who knows? Possibly to mid-summer? I am not showing anything yet, but I should think June at best."

"I see, yeah. So you can take your second-year exams, can't you? That would leave you needing to do one more year after a year's sabbatical, wouldn't it?"

"Ha! In a dream world, perhaps."

"People make their own dream worlds, Margret, and we can make ours. Look, Easter falls in mid-April this year. Let's get married at Easter. You can continue your studies until the end of the academic year. When our baby is born you will have a full year to nurture him," he hesitated, then added, "or her, before you resume your course."

Margret reacted in instinctive manner.

"Charlie Stoker, you stupid big lump, you are mad! Who said anything about marriage? Marriage doesn't come into the equation. I have to decide whether to have a baby or *not*, that is all!"

Charlie ignored the obvious implications, allowing her words to hang in the air before responding with an authority drawn directly from his mother.

"Margret, you are carrying *my* child, *our* child. Let me be clear, I will be a father to my child and I will be a husband to my child's mother. What we have done is to commit a sin in the eyes of the Lord. Only by marriage can we atone for that sin. Only by marriage can we obtain forgiveness from those we love and those who love us. We are both intelligent, sensible people who will make a fine marriage and strong parents. We shall raise children with pride and with honour. I believe we must marry, Margret. Say that you agree."

Margret, head lowered, played with a piece of steak pie on her plate. Then she said:

"Charlie, you are way ahead of me. I am floundering. For the first time in my life I'm not sure that I can handle the situation. My head is in a spin. What I need is a gin!"

Charlie walked to the bar. He lit a cigarette and blew a smoke ring. He fetched a gin and tonic for Margret and a Jamieson's whisky for himself. He said nothing. Margret sipped the gin. She stared across the table at the man who was suddenly displaying a strength of character and a sense of responsibility beyond anything she could ever have expected.

She studied the face of her blond student lover boy, but saw instead a man, a man of honour and purpose: the first man she had ever known for whom she felt respect, admiration, and, God forgive her, love. He had simply cut through the fog of the dilemma and made a decision. Just like that.

"Do you realise what you would be taking on, Charlie?" she asked. "I am not your ordinary girl. I am not a nice girl. I am tall, I'm skinny, I'm ugly and I am wild. I don't care about hurting people. I take no prisoners in any fight—just ask Jennifer Lacey. Or ask anyone who crossed me at school. Ask my bloody family! I am not good enough to clean your boots, Charlie Stoker, and I can't believe you would really want me to be your wife."

She stared at him, provoking no reaction. Then, realising her arms were raised aggressively, she let them drop heavily to the table.

"But…if you honestly believe we can make it work, Big Boy, if you are convinced it is the right thing to do, then, damn it, I will trust you, and I will marry you."

For the third time in the evening tears flowed down Margret Mabey's face, but now they were tears of relief, tears of happiness. Charlie held her and wiped her cheeks with his handkerchief.

She giggled. "I haven't cried since I was about four years old, and tonight I can't stop!"

Charlie smiled, and shrugged.

They agreed that each would inform their parents of the situation and of their decision during the next two days. Charlie would talk to his mother the next day, and Margret intended to go to Clay Hill on the Wednesday. They were both from good Catholic families and neither anticipated too many difficulties once the two families had recovered from the shock of the news.

Then, there was the business of meeting each other's parents before the two families were introduced to each other. It would all have to be arranged very quickly if they hoped to have the wedding in April.

* * *

Charlie decided, rather than wait until the following evening, he would take the bull by the horns. Before going to bed, he told his mother that he was tired, but he had a lot to tell her and would like to chat in the morning. He had no lectures before midday on Tuesdays, which allowed him time to spend with her before leaving home.

Whatever Millie Stoker's true feelings about her son's proposed imminent marriage at the age of nineteen to a person she had not yet met, the only reaction Charlie saw from his mother, as they sat in the upstairs sitting room the next morning, was a look of concerned affection and an application of Stoker common sense.

He had begun by warning her that what followed would be quite a surprise, then had explained in detail how his relationship with Margret had developed. He described her as different from all the other girls he had ever met. She was tall, slim, not at all pretty like Jennifer, but extremely intelligent, articulate, wilful, self-sufficient and independent.

Indeed, he admitted, hers was quite the opposite of his own character. Perhaps that was what had attracted them to each other. In any case, what had happened had happened, and they must face the consequences. He believed the only way to atone for what they knew was a sin in the eyes of the Lord was to marry and to become good parents.

Sorely tempted to beg him to rethink, Millie controlled the impulse. What she was hearing was rational thinking. It was Charles more than Charlie. She felt an inner pride in the strength of character exhibited by her son. Yes, he was only nineteen years old, but she had been hardly more when she had married, had she?

"Charlie," she replied carefully, "In the last few months you have ceased to be a boy. You have grown into a man, a man much like your late father. That has made me very proud. Of course this news today is a shock, but if you are absolutely sure that what you are proposing is the right course for you to take, if you are completely committed to it, then I shall support you without question.

"It is an enormous decision, though, and one that is going to create many headaches for you. It presents you with a mountain of problems for which no one has prepared. For example,

1. You still have to ask for her father's permission. You are both still minors. What if he refuses?

2. You must find a home for you and your wife, one with space for a child.
3. How are you going to pay your way?
4. What of your uncompleted studies? You will need support, at least until you graduate."

Charlie was nodding his head as she listed her points. He replied at once.

"Yes, Mum, I know. About her father, I've still to meet him, but from what Margret has said about their relationship, I suspect he will be keen to offload her. He is a successful solicitor and she thinks that he will have a clear idea of, and will state bluntly, what he considers acceptable procedure.

"We shall find out very soon. I think my meeting with Mr Mabey may also suggest answers to your second and third points. As for our studies, Margret will miss one year, after which she should be able to resume. My situation will depend upon the other decisions. If I need to earn, then I shall have to put my degree on hold, perhaps gain it by evening classes, like Dad. I have to keep an open mind for the moment."

"And the wedding? Is that to be at Enfield?"

"I suppose so. That will all be sorted out within the next week. There's a lot to happen. I can't say anything until I've talked to Mr Mabey."

"Quite. When are you bringing Margret home?"

"I was going to speak to you about that. She is going to her family tomorrow afternoon and back to college on Thursday. I thought maybe she could come here on Friday for the evening and stay the night. She can sleep in my room and I'll sleep on that sofa. Then we can go to Enfield together on Saturday. Would that be alright with you?"

"Yes, of course. It is sensible, son. I look forward to meeting her. I'll make a nice dinner."

Charlie nodded his appreciation and, with a sigh, rose from his chair and approached his mother. He kissed her on the cheek.

"Thanks, Mum, I knew I could rely on you."

Chapter Twelve
Charlie Meets the Mabeys

The following Friday Charlie left his cycle at home and took the bus to the Northern. He had spoken briefly to Margret on the telephone on Wednesday morning, so she knew that she would be welcomed at the Stoker house on Friday evening. Margret had then returned to college on Thursday after spending Wednesday night at Clay Hill.

They met at Holloway Road underground station and travelled together to Amhurst Road. On the tram, she related the story of her trip home. She had left college at midday in order to have plenty of time to talk with her mother and to confirm the suspicions about her condition well before her father arrived home.

The reaction had been startling. Her mother became, in Margret's words, at once a woman transformed. Then, the evening had proved to be quite an amazing experience. For almost the first time in living memory, her mother, tall, timid Mairead Mabey, became not only an ally but an immensely strong ally. It was she who carefully and cunningly led the conversation around to the subject of the marriage proposal, and eventually, inevitably, to the reason for the rushed wedding.

The news was met at first with a cold stare and silence. Then, prompted by his wife to speak, Herbert Mabey demanded to know who the blundering fool was who was prepared to marry the slut.

To Margret's astonishment, Mairead Mabey replied very firmly that such language and such an attitude were neither helpful nor acceptable. They would, she said, appreciate his cooperation in preparing to meet and to approve of their future son-in-law. She believed their daughter had chosen a fine young man.

He was Mr Charles Stoker, of Hackney, son of the late Major Charles Stoker of the Royal Flying Corps and Mrs Mildred Stoker. The probability of a premature birth was unfortunate but a fact of life. They would need to plan for a wedding at Easter.

"Why?" her father had retorted scornfully. "Send her to the convent in Carlow. There is no need to make a public show of this!"

Margret had started to rise from her seat, mouth open to riposte, but she found her mother's hand pressed firmly upon her shoulder, forcing her to remain seated. Instead, it was Mairead who angrily attacked her husband:

"How dare you, Herbert! You are a hypocrite! Have you conveniently forgotten your own passionate youth? Have you forgotten that it is only by the grace of the Lord that we avoided the same situation? You must, and I know you will, do your duty by our daughter. You are to meet Charles on Saturday morning and to discuss everything like a decent prospective father-in-law, and like the upright gentleman that you are."

Herbert Mabey's face had appeared apoplectic, but he had uttered not a word.

* * *

Just before eleven o'clock on the Saturday morning, Betsie welcomed them with a smile and a curtsey at Clay Hill, and whispered to Margret that "Mishter and Mishush" were in the "dworing" room. She took their coats and Margret's small suitcase, and the couple went in to meet the Mabey parents.

The spacious drawing room looked out to the front of the house. It was larger and darker, a more formal room, than the garden room but lit by the warmth of its principle feature, a large open fireplace in which a log fire was burning. Margret's parents were comfortably seated on either side. They rose to greet the visitors and Margret introduced Charlie.

Mairead Mabey struck Charlie as an older, softer version of Margret. Her lined face looked strained, but she produced a warm welcoming greeting and bade them sit on a sofa facing the fire. Her husband Herbert was exactly as expected: sour-faced and curt. He managed to stand and to offer a limp hand to Charlie, several inches taller than he. He nodded at his daughter and sat down again.

Coffee was brought into the room on a tray by a maid not previously seen by Charlie, and there followed polite 'getting-to-know-you' conversation for about half an hour. The subject of the betrothal remained unbroached beyond the initial introductions.

As the clock drew near to midday, however, Mr Mabey, who to this point had hardly uttered more than a few grunts, suddenly stood up and walked over to a cabinet by the wall behind the sofa.

"Let us all enjoy an amontillado before lunch," he said in a deep, authoritative voice that, despite the years in England, had not quite lost its Irish lilt.

"Then, I expect you'll be wanting to have a decent chat, young man. We'll leave the ladies after we've eaten, and talk in my study."

"Well said, dear," Mrs Mabey nodded approvingly.

"Thank God, I'm desperate for a drink!" said Margret.

Lunch was taken in the dining room and consisted of a beef stew with potatoes and dark green cabbage, accompanied by a claret. The wine appeared to be an essential and major part of the meal for both father and daughter. Content as always to go with the crowd, Charlie was happy to accept a glass or two.

Eventually, Herbert Mabey stood up and suggested that he and Charlie enjoy a cigar in his study.

Margret and her mother returned to the drawing room and Charlie followed his host. The study with its heavy furniture was in character with the whole of the house except the airy garden room.

Against one wall was a large mahogany desk, with a wooden armchair in front and a second chair placed to one side; a small leather sofa stood by the window and shelves filled with leather bound books lined the opposite wall. It was the study of a solicitor.

Mabey ushered Charlie into the chair beside the big desk and sat himself heavily into the other, turning the only visible piece of paper face down as he did so. On the corner of the desk was a decanter, two brandy balloons and a wooden box of cigars. He reached for the decanter, pushed the cigar box across the desk and poured a large brandy into each of the two glasses.

"Brandy?" he queried, passing one to Charlie.

"Thank you, sir."

Charlie was learning that life at Clay Hill had its merits. His prospective father-in-law sipped the brandy, then selected and lit a cigar. "Cigar? Help yourself."

"Do you mind if I prefer a cigarette, sir?"

"No, of course, go ahead. So, you lost your father from war wounds, I understand?"

"Not quite, sir." Charlie lit a cigarette from his case. "He was badly injured in the war, but died in an accident in 1926."

"Oh, yes, yes, of course, I remember now, Major Stoker." Mabey fiddled with his cigar, "Wasn't he the flier for whom they held a remembrance service after the riot at Hackney?"

"Yes, that was my father."

Charlie inhaled his cigarette. He had no idea what sort of impression he was making, but it was obvious that his prospective father-in-law solicitor had been researching the Stokers.

"He must have been a fine chap," Herbert Mabey nodded through a cloud of cigar smoke.

"Yes, he was. Did you serve, sir?" Charlie took Mabey slightly by surprise.

"Er, yes. Captain, the Duke of Cambridge's Own Regiment." He studied Charlie over the top of his glass. "I was considerably more fortunate than most, I must say. I went to France for a few months in 1915, but I spent most of my service time at headquarters."

He drank some brandy, then, in as weighty a tone as possible, said:

"Yes, well, perhaps we should get down to business. I must admit, you seem to be a solid young chap, you make a good first impression. But tell me, how do you plan to handle this situation?"

"Handle the situation?" Charlie repeated, "Well, sir, I am here to request your permission for your daughter's hand in marriage."

"Yes, yes, I am aware of that, but you know what I mean. You are both young, and you are both studying. Neither of you is ready for a step like marriage, to say nothing of children. How on earth are you going to provide for her? How are you to complete your studies? What future can you have together with no income? How on earth are you going to bring up a child? Where are you to live? Have you stopped to think about these things at all?"

Mabey's voice grew louder and more forceful with each point until the final one, when he gathered himself and calmed his tone. Charlie was unmoved by the melodrama of the speech. He had been prepared for something similar. In truth, it all sounded a bit rehearsed. His own reply, delivered in his usual relaxed manner, surprised even himself, however.

"I have thought about these things very carefully, Mr Mabey, sir. Our position is, of course, unexpected, but Margret and I have known each other for quite a long time and we get along very well. We are both from good catholic families, but the situation is what it is, and it is in Margret's interest that the wedding take place as soon as possible.

"She is a born academic and she must have the opportunity to complete her studies. She can finish this year to June and take her intermediate examination, then take a year out from university to give birth and to nurture our child. By September 1931, she could resume and complete her course.

"I shall also complete this year's studies, but then it will be necessary for me to earn a living. I should aim to gain my degree at evening classes in the next few years. We shall of course need somewhere to live, but I know my mother will be prepared to find us accommodation if we ask her. As for income, I have confidence that I can and shall earn a living, although I have not yet considered exactly how. There is always the shoe repair business, of course."

"Shoe repair? Shoe repairs? What have you to do with that?"

"My father set up a business after the war, when he was unable to resume his career."

"Quite, but that was a one-man business and someone is doing that job now, aren't they? Anyway, that is no career for an educated man."

"My father was an educated man, sir."

"Quite, quite. I meant no offence, but you must surely seek a proper career."

The blustering solicitor paused, then said: "How old are you exactly, Charles?"

Charlie grinned and shrugged. "I shall be twenty in November, sir, and if you'll forgive me, I am known as Charlie, not Charles. My father was Charles."

The older man blinked and played with his cigar.

"You are a remarkably self-confident and clear-thinking young man for nineteen, Charlie," he said. "I must say, I am most impressed. And you are articulate. I begin to understand what my daughter sees in you. My Margret is not an easy person—and I do not always handle her well. She is intelligent, fiery, independent and difficult. Yet, I think if anyone can handle her, it may well be you."

Reaching for the piece of paper on the desk, he turned it over, glanced quickly down the page and then replaced it face down. He fussed with his cigar and sipped more brandy.

Eventually, he said:

"Charlie, have you considered a legal career? You have an instinct for talking to people, and I feel it could be the right direction for you."

"Honestly, sir, no. I am studying physics and maths."

"That's irrelevant! All education is good education. You are the right type, Charlie. I like you. If you are to study at evening classes, study law. I can find a place for you and I will train you to be my clerk. My clerk is the most important person in the office.

"Once you have learned the basics, the work becomes interesting and demanding, and you would be rewarded accordingly. As for a home, we can make space for you here at Clay Hill. We have two rooms unused. Together with Margret's bedroom, they can be adapted to make a small suite for you to start married life. Then, after a couple of years, we can help you to find your own house nearby. What do you say?"

"It is a very generous offer, sir," Charlie replied.

He needed time to think. He took another cigarette from his case and lit it, smiling as he waved away the smoke.

"I'm tempted to say yes right away, sir, but things seem to be moving so fast, maybe that wouldn't be wise. Do you mind if I think about it for a day or two and talk it over with my mother?"

He tapped ash from the cigarette, then laughed.

"Do I take this offer as meaning I have your permission to purchase an engagement ring, sir?"

"Ha! Ha! Yes, quite so! Yes, indeed." Herbert Mabey emptied his brandy balloon and fiddled with his cigar. Then, as if making a sudden decision, he reached out to shake Charlie's hand. "You're a fine young man, Charlie, the right stuff. Good luck to you."

Charlie shook hands, smiling, but not speaking.

* * *

Millie, having shown her usual calm in dealing with the bombshell of Charlie's news and the consequent visit of the girl Margret, allowed her anxieties to surface once they had left the house. In her head she admired her son's moral strength and his cool decision-making; but her heart told her that the proposed marriage would be a disaster. There was something about that girl, a look, an attitude, something she sensed that caused unease. She resolved to talk at once with Father Peter.

As ever, the wise old priest became witness to her true feelings. As ever, he comforted her and guided her to a state of acceptance and to a more moderate view of the likely outcome.

Yes, her son and his chosen wife-to-be had sinned, he acknowledged, but it was not the Lord's wrath they should fear. They were good Catholics. The Lord would hear their confessions, would forgive and absolve them. Then, naturally, he himself would be delighted to conduct the ceremony, although he expected the bride's family to approach Fr. Tuohy at Enfield. Fr. Tuohy would hold a similar view, he felt sure.

He leaned closer to her.

"If I were to admit, dear Millie," he whispered, holding her hand, "how many of my most devout parishioners had similarly sinned over the years, the numbers would stagger you. No," he concluded sorrowfully, "the price such couples must invariably pay is in the strain that this life places upon them as a consequence of their actions."

In this respect, he observed more brightly, young Charlie was better equipped than most to cope.

"Charlie is an exceptionally mature young man. Your fears are the natural fears of a mother about to see her only son move on the next stage of his life."

Addressing her greatest fear, the priest said:

"I have not yet met Miss Mabey, but this was your first meeting. It is natural that the girl should appear apprehensive. Give her time, give yourself time to get to know her. This is not a time of sadness for you, Millie, those days are past. This is wonderful news. After so many years of suffering such terrible losses, of seeing the constant depletion of your family, you are, by the grace of God, at last to see it grow again."

* * *

Charlie, having now reached a conclusion about his immediate future, sat with his mother once again in the upstairs sitting room to report on his visit to the Mabeys. Typically, he expressed no judgemental opinion of his wife-to-be's family. He said only that Mrs Mabey was tall, like Margret, and Mr Mabey was an Irish lawyer, thickset of build with a rather florid complexion. He then told Millie in detail of the events of the day, especially of the interview in the solicitor's study.

If he expected his mother to object to the idea of any interference in his studies, she, as so often, surprised him.

"What a remarkably generous offer!" she exclaimed. "It sounds like the ideal way forward for you, Charlie. You know I believe it imperative that you gain a degree and I wanted you to follow your father. But a law degree would bestow even more honour on his memory. He would be very proud of you, Charlie, as indeed should I. But how do you feel about it yourself?"

Charlie shrugged and grinned.

"I guess we all feel the same about it. It is a generous offer. The only trouble is, I don't think I'm going to enjoy the first year or two very much, Mum. I have a feeling that the atmosphere in Enfield may be somewhat too heavy, to say the least. I suspect Margret's brother Harry is going to resent my presence. He is the first-born, and very conscious of the fact, I understand. I shan't have any peace of mind or sense of freedom until we can move out of Clay Hill and settle in our own home."

"Well, that will all be up to you, my son, but you'll handle it well, I have no doubt."

Thus, both families seemed to accept the inevitable, and so commenced a whirl of activity. Within a week, Charlie had presented Margret with an engagement ring, a tiny solitaire diamond in a gold filigree setting, purchased with ten pounds from his savings account. Millie Stoker had exchanged visits with the Mabeys, and arrangements had been agreed for a marriage ceremony at the Church of Our Lady of Mount Carmel, Enfield, on the Wednesday of the week after Easter. A small private reception would be held at Clay Hill for the two families and a few chosen friends.

On the Monday after this was arranged, Charlie, eating his lunchtime sandwiches with Bobby in a corner of the refectory, asked his bewildered friend to be his best man.

"W-w-what are you talking about? Y-you know I w-want you to be my best man, b-but that won't be until n-ext year!" stammered the startled Bobby.

"No, Bobby, not me your best man, you my best man. I am getting married on the Wednesday after Easter. I am marrying Margret Mabey, and I want you to be my best man."

Bobby's mouth fell open and his half-eaten sandwich dropped into his lap. He stared at his friend in utter bewilderment. Charlie, a twinkle in his eye, shrugged and lit a cigarette.

"Y-y-you and M-Margret M-Mabey!" exclaimed Bobby, rediscovering his voice after a lapse of some seconds, and desperately trying to control his stammer. "B-b-but h-how on earth has that happened? We d-on't s-see her off-en, do we?"

"Well, no, *we* don't, Bobby, but I do."

Charlie sighed.

"I've been seeing her since last August, and it's just sort of happened." He inhaled, then shrugged.

Bobby often gave the appearance of being a bit slow, perhaps because of his stammer and his thick spectacles; but nothing could be farther from the truth. He looked hard at Charlie.

"'I-I-it sort of...?' Blimey, you've p-put her—!'" he stopped mid-sentence, his finger pointing at Charlie and wagging up and down accusingly as he sought affirmation.

"Yeah."

"B-b-bloody damn, Charlie!"

"Bloody damn indeed, pal, but that's how it is. I'm getting married and are you going to be my best man?"

"B-bloody damn yes, Charlie. Y-you know I'll be p-proud to stand by your side."

He grabbed Charlie's hand and pumped it up and down between his two mechanic's hands, his face bright red and his eyes glowing with pride.

Charlie said: "It'll be a quiet affair, of course, mainly just the two families and very close friends; but you'll bring Daphne, won't you? Jennifer is to be maid of honour."

"Is she? Yes, D-Daphne'll be p-pleased and excited! Gosh me, Charlie!"

* * *

Margret had the far more delicate task of explaining the situation to Jennifer Lacey. She knew Jennifer far better than anyone, and she was fully aware that she had, the previous summer, quite deliberately destroyed any lingering chance of a relationship developing between her friend and Charlie, not that that had ever been seriously likely.

Anyway, as she explained bluntly in the privacy of Jennifer's room in the Lacey home, Jennifer had quite clearly tired of him six months earlier. Having paraded him around as her trophy for a term at college, she had made no attempt to tie him to her physically; and she had discarded him at her party in the same way that they had always discarded boys. So Margret had felt no shame in having picked up the poor thing and bedded him.

What had transpired subsequently, she told the wide-eyed Jennifer, had shocked her beyond belief. She had regarded Big Boy as just another plaything. He had been a complete innocent. She had had to teach him everything about making love; but then he had become extraordinarily proficient at it. So much so, that she had begun to ache for him. Then, the weekend her parents went away, she had broken her golden rule. She had taken him to bed on her sixth day. Statistically, she argued, it should not have mattered, but the Lord had decided otherwise. She had become pregnant. She was now with child. She was to marry Charlie Stoker at Easter, and Jennifer was to be her maid-of-honour, and her support, as always.

"But…but," Jennifer struggled to put her reaction into words. Margret was right to say they had both treated Charlie Stoker as a plaything. But never could she have foreseen this outcome. Their whole world had been turned upside down. She wanted to say the situation was ridiculous, it was impossible, but her actual words were:

"Of course, Margret, if it is what you want, then I shall support you. If it is what you think is right—and you are happy, then I am happy for you. You know I shall always be here for you."

"Yes, my little pearl, I know. This is not what I want. This is the world we live in, and conformity is the price we must pay."

She took her friend into her arms and hugged her tightly.

"You will make a beautiful maid-of-honour."

"Yes," replied Jennifer through her tears.

Chapter Thirteen
Marriage and Enfield

Charles Horace Stoker, aged nineteen, was married to twenty-year-old Margret Cavendish Mabey in the Catholic Church of Our Lady of Mt Carmel and St George at Enfield on April 10th 1930.

Millie Stoker had told Stephen Collick of the impending event, and was delighted when he indicated that he would very much like to attend the wedding. He said he would be proud to escort Millie for the day. He was acquainted with the Mabey parents—had met them once or twice and believed they were well thought of locally—but he did not know the children.

The occasion, indeed the whole day, proved to be a great success. The Lanchester duly arrived at Amhurst Road in the morning. The ceremony was to be concelebrated by Fr Denis Tuohy and, by special invitation, Fr Peter O'Rahilly from Hackney. Father Tuohy, before being granted his own parish, had served under the guidance of Father Peter for some time, and so was known to Millie and Charlie.

Father Peter arrived early at Amhurst Road and was waiting with the Stokers when Stephen Collick arrived. Together, they all drove to the church at Enfield. Bobby, the best man, was waiting outside the church when they arrived, and the two young men took their places near the altar to await the arrival of the bride.

They both wore grey morning suits and Bobby's wild red hair was newly trimmed and neatly parted. He looked strangely smart, but Charlie, of course, tall and well-built, appeared far the more comfortable in the formal dress.

Looking around, the groom momentarily glimpsed the bridal party entering the church, with Margret looking stunningly elegant on her father's arm. The bride was wearing a sleek white Chantilly lace-trimmed silk gown that perfectly suited her tall, slim frame. As she joined him at the altar, he was reminded of the silk-clad angel of the Lacey party and his smile broadened to a grin.

Behind her, in a gown of similar style but in pink silk with a corsage of spring flowers, Jennifer looked straight ahead, beaming the smile of a woman fully aware of her ability to draw the eyes of men. Her light brown hair, shining golden in the beam of sunlight directed at her through a stained-glass window, was no longer in ringlets but styled in the latest fashion with a deep finger wave leading down to pin curls. She was quite beautiful.

Miss Margret Mabey became Mrs Margret Stoker to the delight and relief of her mother, and to the evident satisfaction of her father, who felt he had made a significant gain in acquiring his new trainee solicitor. His feeling of satisfaction was enhanced considerably by the knowledge that Mrs Millie Stoker, the groom's mother, was accompanied by no other than the Hon. Stephen Collick, younger brother of Lord Collick. He had not imagined for a moment that his new son-in-law would be so well-connected.

A wedding breakfast was served in the dining room of the Clay Hill residence, and was enjoyed by a total of eighteen people: the bride and groom, the Mabey and Lacey families, Millie and Stephen, Bobby and Daphne and the two priests.

Four speeches were made: a stiff and rather formal performance by the father of the bride, a relaxed but responsible reply by the groom, and a sparkling effort by the best man, Mr Robert Bruce. With the aid of alcoholic lubrication, Bobby delivered with barely a hesitation a short but hilarious speech built around a fictitious story of an attempt by Charlie to win the cycling club's annual road race. It was warmly received by all present.

The final speech was a brief but carefully considered address by Father Peter, giving thanks to the hosts for the wonderful lunch, thanks to the Lord for the beautiful weather, and fatherly advice and his blessing to the newly-weds.

Following lunch, everybody was invited to enjoy the further hospitality of their Mabey hosts in the garden room, the terrace and the garden.

By late afternoon, not surprisingly, Bobby was considerably inebriated. On the terrace, well supported by Daphne, he entertained everyone with excerpts from Gilbert and Sullivan operas and popular music hall melodies in his rich baritone voice. An accomplished piano accompaniment was supplied by Jennifer's mother, Mrs Sarah Lacey.

At about seven o'clock, a breeze sprang up and the evening grew suddenly cool. The garden was vacated and people spread about the house, chatting. Charlie took the opportunity to show his mother the three-roomed suite that had been created for Margret and himself from Margret's bedroom and two adjoining rooms.

Millie professed herself impressed, although her tone, Charlie felt, lacked conviction. Towards nine o'clock, she indicated that it was time for her to leave. Father Peter was looking very tired and had a heavy schedule for the next day, she said.

Bobby, slightly the worse for wear and somewhat disappointed that Charlie still appeared sober, hugged the groom and his bride before being accompanied home by the loyal Daphne.

On the train to Harringay, the two reviewed their day. It had been a great success, Daphne proclaimed eagerly. Only two people, she thought, appeared to show no particular enthusiasm for the event.

"Did you see those brothers of Margret's, Harry and Terence?" she asked incredulously. "The older one, the one who's a solicitor, he seemed to spend the day cultivating his air of superiority. The only times he looked interested in anything was when he was talking to that Mr Collick or else when he was ogling Jennifer Lacey. I didn't speak to him at all, but every time I saw him, he looked bored. And the younger one, the student, Terence, well, he seemed to be in a permanent sulk, didn't he?"

Bobby roused himself to reply.

"Yeah, well, they're Margret's f-family, aren't they? I th-think they're all a bit odd. I mean, Margret's not your usual woman, is she? She's not exactly easy to be with, is she? Only, d-d-don't say anything like that to Charlie!"

"No, of course not, silly!" She gave him a gentle slap.

"But you're right, they were a bit of a funny lot, her family, weren't they?"

Bobby busied himself removing and studiously cleaning his spectacles. When he was satisfied with his work, he replaced them with a little grunt of satisfaction. Then he put his arm around Daphne's shoulders. He squeezed gently and whispered,

"W-we're alright, though!"

* * *

Charlie and Margret, thoroughly exhausted and mightily relieved, travelled the next morning by train from Victoria station to Eastbourne to enjoy a relaxed week's honeymoon before resuming their studies. They planned to take their respective examinations in June, after which Charlie would commence his legal career.

The first few weeks of the summer term at the Northern were mostly devoid of lectures and were devoted to revision leading up to the examinations. Charlie, confidently doing most of his revision at Clay Hill or in his old room at Amhurst Road, attended the college for only a few hours each week.

Bobby Bruce, on the other hand, for whom these were to be his final examinations, was there daily. This was, for him, despite his friend's words of comfort and reiterated votes of confidence, an increasingly anxious and stressful time.

By the time of Charlie's marriage, any remaining strands of reserve in their friendship had been erased. Bobby attributed the establishment of his relationship with Daphne to Charlie's introduction, and he felt deeply privileged to have been asked to be his friend's best man.

Charlie, in turn, was greatly moved by Bobby's obvious commitment to their friendship; and he was proud of Bobby's public performance on the wedding day. They were now each other's close confidant, the brother neither had ever had. Their

Saturday morning swim and chat sessions continued and, although Margret and Daphne had little in common, the four got together as couples as often as possible.

Margret also concentrated on preparation for her examinations. She studied at home, commuting to LSE only on an occasional basis. After a thorough medical examination by Dr Leghorn, the family doctor, within days of her mother being apprised of her situation in January, the progress of her pregnancy had been monitored regularly. Being pregnant seemed hardly to affect her, and she sat the exams in fine spirits in the June of 1930.

"Really, it has all been rather a cakewalk," she professed perkily to Charlie.

But then, towards the end of June, with the exams behind her, her condition became suddenly bothersome. She awoke one morning to find her abdomen clearly distended and her ankles badly swollen. The business was now far less of a cakewalk. It was a most unwelcome shock. Her good humour rapidly evaporated as her irritation grew at the limitations suddenly placed upon her mobility: by the bouts of perspiration that caused her clothes to stick to her body; by the back pain and the sore breasts.

Margret was a stormy petrel; at times she could be a wildcat. She resented the abrupt loss of her athleticism and her svelte figure. For the first time, she felt no inclination to romp (her term for all sexual activity). Resentment and irritation quickly turned her tongue into a lash that whipped—often mercilessly—whomever happened to be nearby.

The Mabey household, if not immune to her rages, was certainly accustomed to them. They generally made themselves scarce when Margret went wild; with the exception of her father, who tended to reciprocate with outbursts of his own. This had, in years gone by, led to many verbal battles and more than once to a fierce exchange of blows, invariably more damaging to Herbert Mabey.

Charlie had been clearly warned of her 'wild Irish blood' when he had first proposed marriage. Margret had told him of various incidents from her past when her intemperate outbursts had led her to cause pain and injury to those in her path.

He himself had witnessed an occasional hint of her fire at the Victoria Tavern, but it had invariably been merely a flashing eye and a sharp put down for the unsuspecting recipient: a casual assertion of her intellectual superiority over the assembled company.

The occasional moments of tension in their own relationship were invariably dispelled by the Stoker smile and a shrug; or, if absolutely necessary, a few minutes of separation and a cigarette, followed by the Stoker smile. Indeed, it was Charlie's skill at removing the heat from a crisis, his knack of remaining calm at moments of stress, that was the aspect of his character most respected by Margret, and, if truth be told, what most endeared him to her.

And he had endeared himself to her, she realised in a rare moment of calm reflection. Her Big Boy, her plaything, had completely wrecked her games. He had turned her world upside down; and instead of hating him for it, she found herself strangely contented. She felt gratitude for this transformation of her life, for his having created a living, breathing child inside her. He had actually done that! Despite the pain and the damned inconvenience of pregnancy, she told herself, she felt more warmth for this man, her husband, Charlie Stoker, than she had ever felt for anyone in the world—except, perhaps, dear Jennifer. Certainly more than she would have conceived it possible to feel for any man.

Chapter Fourteen
The World Upside Down

Charlie found himself working in the office of Cavendish, Brigham, Mabey sooner than he expected. Shortly after the wedding, Herbert Mabey suggested he spend three hours per day learning the routines of the office and getting the general feel of legal work. Each morning, therefore, he left the house at eight o'clock for the pleasant walk to Church Street.

This office experience, while still adjusting to married life at Clay Hill, and in addition to preparing for and then sitting his examinations, meant that Charlie had little time for other activities during the summer of 1930. Never one to be shy of work, the young man threw himself willingly into learning the daily routines and completing all the tasks demanded of him.

His relaxed and considerate attitude was welcomed and appreciated by the main office staff. This included the stern-faced Miss Pettit, spinster, keen gardener and office bookkeeper; Charlotte Caldecot, Mr Mabey's prim and plain private secretary; and Anne, the office typist, a quick-witted girl, pretty with a tendency to plumpness.

His enthusiasm, however, was not appreciated by all. The Stoker smile and shrug, he found, were of little avail against the resentful condescension of his brother-in-law, the young solicitor, Mr Herbert Lionel Cavendish Mabey Jnr.

Margret's elder brother's attitude towards his sister's husband had been somewhat frosty from their first meeting. Harry treated him as an intruder. The Mabey parents had welcomed Charlie warmly, but in such an obviously dysfunctional household he was not surprised to feel antipathy from his wife's former abuser.

He soon learned, however, when invited to enjoy a late evening whisky in his father-in-law's study, (a whisky that became the greater part of a bottle shared between the two of them) that Harry's antipathy stemmed not just from Charlie's relationship with his sister, but from the potential effect of his arrival upon Harry's own career.

By the time he revealed this information, Herbert Mabey was quite drunk: drunk to the point of becoming maudlin. His son, he confided, was a great disappointment. He had a degree in law, but that achievement had been made possible only by 'packages passed quietly behind screens' (this phrase accompanied by knowing nods). Harry, in his father's words, was lacking both any proper grasp of law and the slightest business acumen.

His face redder than ever, Mabey declared that he regarded his son as a necessary encumbrance rather than a future partner. His bloodshot eyes leaked a tear as he added miserably,

"What's more, I can't see his young brother being any better. The only one of the three of them with any real spark is the girl, and she is a virago who refuses to have anything to do with her father or the legal profession."

The Church Street office was filled with an atmosphere of nervous unease most of the time. Harry was not the only problem. His father was a self-important bully who drank too much and could not hold his liquor. On many mornings, Mabey Senior arrived with a bad hangover and an equally bad humour, or he simply did not appear until much later in the day. On those days, decisions made in his absence by members of staff would invariably be irritably countermanded upon his arrival.

Embarrassingly, he was never rude to Charlie. He added to his son's aggravations by treating his new son-in-law with excessive consideration and politeness.

On a Thursday afternoon at the end of July, Charlie enjoyed a short tea break chatting with Anne and Miss Pettit. The newspapers were still full of news of the earthquake near Naples that had caused thousands of deaths a few days earlier, and of Stalin boasting of the success of his purges; but the day's biggest headline had concerned the maiden flight of the R101 airship across the Atlantic.

Charlie related how he and Margret had marvelled at the sight of the massive machine as it passed majestically over Clay Hill some nine months earlier. Anne said it was her dream to go up in it.

The conversation was halted by the sudden appearance of Charlotte Caldecot from Herbert Mabey's office. Mr Stoker was to drop whatever he was doing and to attend Mr Mabey at once.

Charlie moved quickly to find his father-in-law standing, fidgeting, behind his large dark oak desk. Without any preamble, and in a state of considerable ill-humour, Mabey barked: "We must return to Clay Hill at once, dammit! Margret—some difficulty, it seems. The child—some problem, you see. Come, my motor is at the door!"

He strode around the desk, heading for the door and brushing past Charlie before he could ask a question. Once in the car, Mabey explained that the doctor had been called to the house when Margret experienced sudden pain soon after Charlie had left for the office.

The baby was not due for another two weeks but, according to his wife's report, contractions had already begun. The pains were intense and Margret's blood pressure was unusually high. The doctor was now suggesting that she be moved to the hospital for more careful monitoring but he wanted her husband's consent before taking any action.

They rushed into the house to be greeted by an anxious-looking Mairead Mabey. She bade them slow down and be calm, although, in truth, only her husband needed calming. Charlie was his usual self. His mother-in-law explained that Margret's pains had subsided somewhat and she was now sleeping, if only for the moment. However, Alex was waiting to speak to them in the garden room.

Alexander Leghorn MD was a family friend who had tended to the Mabeys' medical needs for many years. He and Herbert Mabey were both committee members of the local golf club and the two wives played cards together. Charlie had met the doctor on one or two occasions when he had called to carry out routine checks on Margret.

He had found the G.P. to be good company, a bluff, stocky Scotsman with a fine sense of humour and a hint of a retained

Edinburgh accent. On this day, however, the medical man, his demeanour serious, greeted both men with a short handshake: but he addressed himself solely to Charlie.

"Now, there's no need to fret yourse'f, young man, everything will be fine, but there are a couple of things to make clear. Margret has now been in labour for six or seven hours. I have conducted an initial examination, and the baby sounds as if it is in distress: it has manoeuvred itself into a bad position.

"This is causing a great deal of pain to your wife's back. I told her that I feel it calls for a delivery by Caesarean section, but she became agitated and refused to entertain the possibility. Under the circumstances, I think the sooner I can move them to Chase Side, carry out a more intensive examination and get the bairn delivered, the better for both of them. I should like to do that at once, and with your consent I shall send for the ambulance straight away," he proffered a form and a pen.

Charlie shrugged.

"Well, yes, of course you have my consent if you think it is the right thing to do. After all, I'm new at this, you are the expert." He smiled at the doctor and signed the document where indicated.

Alex Leghorn moved swiftly into action. Within twenty minutes, Margret, awake again and groaning with obvious pain, was lifted down the stairs, into the ambulance and away to the Cottage Hospital. The family members were instructed to wait in the house for a call after a fuller investigation.

"Shall we all have a quiet cup of tea?" suggested Mairead Mabey once the ambulance had left. "We'll take it in the garden room, I think." She shooed the two men towards the garden room, then hurried to the kitchen to organise Betsie.

Herbert dropped heavily into an armchair with a grunt and a "Well, well!" but said no more. Charlie stood by the open French door, staring at the garden.

"Oh dear," Mairead sighed, re-joining them a few minutes later, "I feared something was not right this morning. Margret has been quite agreeable just lately—forgive me, Charlie, I don't mean that to sound offensive."

"Not at all, I know what you mean. She's not easy!"

"No, certainly not, but recently she has been, as I said, quite pleasant and amenable company. You have been a remarkably calming influence upon her. But this morning it was back to the old ways of screaming and shouting. She was cursing her condition, she cursed the child within her, and she was even cursing you for creating it."

"Well that was a fifty-fifty operation, I should say," replied Charlie with a shrug, attempting to lighten the conversation.

"Ha-hmmph!" grunted his father-in-law, fetching a glower from his wife.

"Yes, quite!" Mairead wrung her hands.

Charlie took a cigarette from his case and inhaled slowly. Betsie entered with the tea trolley and scuttled out again. Mairead waited a few minutes before pouring tea for the three of them. She turned back to face Charlie.

"What I wonder, though, is whether—you see, they have taken her off so quickly—whether, if you were with her, she may be more reasonable and more amenable to Alex's preference for a Caesarean section. I should think it by far the wiser course. You see, Margret's build is very much like my own. I had three children effortlessly and she no doubt believes that anything I can do, she can outdo. But something has gone seriously wrong in her case, there is no doubt."

"Ye-es, I'm beginning to understand that. It is worth a try, of course, but Margret is a vessel not easily turned, as my grandfather would have said. Still, if I can be allowed near her, I'll try my best to change her mind."

"I shall make sure you can get to her!"

Herbert Mabey erupted out of his chair with the decisiveness of a bull. "Come. I'll drive you there now."

Mairead reached across to lay her hand on her husband's arm.

"Wait a moment, dear. Perhaps we should finish our tea before you rush off? It is not yet an hour since they left. Why don't you call Alex or Matron Matteson on the telephone and inform them of our idea?"

Mabey uttered a disgruntled acquiescence and left the room. Charlie, watching, was coming to the conclusion that his wife's assessment of her mother was uncharacteristically misplaced.

Yes, Mairead was quiet and self-effacing, but in the time he had been acquainted with her she had never appeared weak. She was most certainly not, as Margret had described her, 'a mouse, content to do her husband's bidding'.

* * *

Matron Matteson ushered Charlie into her little office and bade him sit on the cushioned wheel-back chair behind the door. She was a well-built woman of his mother's age with a cultivated air of authority. She sat down on a matching chair facing him from behind the neat desk before addressing him.

"It is good that you are here, Mr Stoker. Mr Mabey spoke to me on the telephone, as you know, but you are the only person with whom we can discuss this. Your wife is resting quietly at the moment and her contractions are quite regular at about ten-minute intervals. They appear to have remained like that for several hours now, which is not unusual. But the degree of pain she is suffering is exceptional, due in part to the foetus becoming badly positioned and pressing on a nerve. There are now also clear signs of foetal distress. I believe Dr Leghorn has already explained this to you," she lifted a paper from the desk, "and I see he has obtained your consent to deliver by Caesarean section if necessary."

Charlie nodded, "Yes."

"However," she continued purposefully, "Mrs Stoker is objecting fiercely to the suggestion of any surgical incision. Dr Leghorn has asked me to confirm that you understand that we have your full consent to take whatever action may be necessary to protect the lives of mother and child."

Charlie nodded. He put his hand inside his jacket and withdrew his cigarette case, waving it slowly in the air to give himself time to think. "Do you mind?" he asked.

"No, go ahead." She pushed an ashtray across the desk to within his reach.

Charlie lit and inhaled, slowly exhaling the resultant cloud sideways, away from the desk.

"Alex Leghorn asked me for permission to move Margret here," he said deliberately. "He talked about Margret's objections—she wants to give birth naturally like other women—but I thought I was here to talk to Margret, to change her mind."

"I suspect her condition is determining that we have no option, Mr Stoker. Dr Leghorn and my staff are working now to attempt to correct or to improve the foetal position, but I have to say that matters are reaching the critical stage. If they are unsuccessful now, the baby's life—and possibly the mother's—will be at risk unless we take immediate action."

She took a deep breath.

"Let me be blunt, sir. Even with a Caesarean section this birth will be dangerous. We are talking about the lives of your wife and child!"

Charlie blanched. He crushed out the half-smoked cigarette.

"I see. Well, you have my consent, just do what's right! Can I see her?"

"Not just now, I am afraid, Mr Stoker. The doctor has set a deadline for the control of the foetal distress symptoms and she has a nurse with her the whole time."

She glanced at her watch.

"Oh, dear me, time is rushing by. Look, I am under a little pressure just at the moment. We have a more comfortable room just next door, let me take you there and arrange for a cup of tea for you while I go to see what the position is. If I am further delayed, I shall ensure that you are informed of the situation."

The matron led him to a room next door, in which a small side table stood under the window between a pair of upholstered easy chairs. A newspaper and some magazines lay on the table. Charlie shrugged, lit a cigarette and picked up the paper. A trainee nurse soon appeared with a tray of tea and some biscuits. Then he was left to his thoughts.

The window looked out upon a bed of neatly trimmed shrubs and small trees bordering the front drive. It was a pleasant, lazy summer's evening, the afternoon's blue sky now made pale by wispy cirrus clouds. Charlie stared upwards and pondered on how his life had been transformed.

Six short months ago he had been floating aimlessly along with a physics degree as his only goal. And now look at him: a married man, about to be a father, and learning to be a solicitor. In addition to his office work, there would be a great deal of studying to do. It was all very well for his father-in-law to think he could easily gain a law degree, Charlie realised he was in for a tough time for some years. He would have to really knuckle down to it.

Of course, they'd be okay once Margret had qualified. Then they could buy a house of their own, a mile or two clear of the family. He smiled to himself. He would be there for their son. Unlike his own father, he would see him grow up. It never occurred to Charlie for more than brief moments that the child would not be a boy.

His reverie was disturbed by the voice of a junior nurse, who entered carrying a tray on which lay a plate filled with a cold meat salad, a glass of milk and two slices of bread and butter.

"Matron asked me to tell you that things had sort of settled down with your wife, and, now, Mrs Stoker's contractions are becoming more frequent. She said you were to eat some supper and relax. It should all be over in the next hour."

Charlie smiled and thanked her. He devoured the food. He had not realised how hungry he was. He lit a cigarette and blew the smoke out slowly, in rings. Unsurprisingly, Jennifer came into his thoughts. She had taught him that trick. Jennifer, with her posing. She was, without doubt, a stunningly beautiful girl…woman! She would be twenty in a month or so… She had looked absolutely outstanding at the wedding.

Yet, somehow, he had never felt sexually aroused by Jennifer. It took little more than a few seconds for Margret to cause him embarrassment when she chose to, but never Jennifer. All he had ever received was an apprehensive proffered cheek or pouted lips. Not that it had bothered him at all. He responded eagerly enough to Margret's enthusiastic romping because it was exciting, pure and simple. But was it important? Well, yes, if you understood the consequences, if you wanted to produce children. But for daily thrills, he could take it or leave it.

Charlie Stoker could happily fill his time in other ways. Perhaps that's how Jennifer Lacey felt? He had not seen much of her since the exams. To the best of his knowledge, she had not had a special boyfriend since he had learned to drink

Jamieson's with her father. She still had all her friends, of course. Daphne worked and studied with her, but Daphne now spent her free time with Bobby. Jennifer saw Margret quite often, usually on Wednesday afternoons, when the chemist's was closed. Like Bobby and Daphne, Jennifer was awaiting the results of her examinations. She was helping her father in the pharmacy and anticipating a good result, no doubt...

"Mr Stoker?" The gentle shaking of his shoulder and the Lancastrian voice of Matron Matteson roused Charlie from deep sleep in the easy chair.

"Crikey! I was out cold, forgive me."

He dragged himself into an upright sitting position and saw the matron and Alex Leghorn standing in front of him.

"Is everything alright?"

It was the doctor who replied.

"Margret gave birth to a baby boy a short time ago, Charlie. Due to some late complications when the baby again signalled severe distress, it was necessary to deliver by Caesarean section. Margret is now sleeping but she will be fine when she recovers."

He paused for a moment, keeping his eyes steadily on the young man in front of him.

"Your baby boy, a big baby, weighing over nine pounds, appeared to be quite still at the moment of delivery. The midwife assisting me made every possible effort, using all means known, to encourage him to breathe and to cry out, but to no avail. Sadly, Charlie, he was unable to make it. We lost him."

Charlie, now wide awake, asked in a rising tone: "What do you mean, you lost him? What happened? Are you saying our baby is dead?"

The matron moved quickly to his side and rested her hand on his shoulder. "Now, calm yourself, Mr Stoker," she spoke with practised gentleness, "let me fetch something to help."

She left the room to return almost immediately carrying a small tray on which stood a half-full decanter and two glasses of brandy. She pressed one glass into Charlie's hand and the doctor gathered the other from the tray. Charlie drank a little brandy and lit a cigarette.

"The bairn was stillborn, Charlie," said Alex deliberately. "Although it can happen at any delivery, this was quite unforeseen and completely beyond our control. When we lifted him from the womb, he was still. I know it has to be a terrible shock for you at this moment, but the important thing for you to hang on to is that Margret is fine. She will need a week or two to recover from the surgery, but she will be able to resume her normal life and to have plenty more children."

He swallowed some brandy.

"You are both very young and you have plenty of time. Tragically, old chap, we never know when this may occur or why. Birth is ever a risky business. A quarter of all the children we bring into this world do not survive infancy; and something like five in every hundred are stillborn. Only the Lord knows why."

Charlie, his face pale, drained the glass and stood up, towering above the two of them. He nodded at Alex and said in a flat tone:

"I understand. Can I see my wife now?"

"I can let you see her briefly, Mr Stoker."

This from the matron. "But she is sleeping now, and she will remain so all night. Of course, you will be in need of a good night's sleep, also. Dr Leghorn has suggested he drive you home when you have looked in on Margret."

"Thank you."

The lovely summer evening had faded to a still night by the time they left the little hospital. Charlie saw it as a curtain being drawn over the events of the day; perhaps also a door closing on the events of a year that had already utterly changed his life; and now, he felt, had so aged him.

Alex, who had ensured that the matron lace Charlie's brandy with a sleeping draught, escorted the young man into the house and saw him to his bed. He then spent an hour explaining the situation to, and consoling Margret's parents over a brandy or two, before going home to reflect upon the disaster he had been instrumental in bringing upon yet another young couple.

The sleeping draught had made Charlie very drowsy, but nevertheless, when Alex left the room he climbed out of bed and went to the window. He felt weighed down, enshrouded by a dark fog, the same dense cloud he had known when standing at the top of the basement staircase just four years earlier. But that had not been the first time, had it? He had been there long before that. His mind drifted back.

His earliest recollection of the feeling was when he was small, when Granddad Ockie had vanished. Then his laughing father disappeared to France, only to return—after what seemed like a lifetime—a completely different person. After that, his grandmother had just faded away…and Granddad George at the bottom of the stairs… Then, in 1926, *that* day, *that* terrible day… And now this…

He was not yet twenty, was this all that life was supposed to be?

Unaware of the tears rolling down his cheeks, he stared through the window and screamed voicelessly to the heavens.

'Why me? Why do you continually torture me? Is this to be the pattern of my whole life? Must death strike at my heart every couple of years? Is this what you have ordained for Charles Horace Stoker? Why did you bar my parents from giving me a brother? Why have you now taken away my son? What have I done to deserve this? Why is it a crime punishable by death to be loved by Charlie Stoker?'

Tears flooded his face and ran down his neck as the torrent of questions was thrown at Almighty God. But God's face through the dark cloud was represented by the kind, weeping eyes of old Father Peter O'Rahilly.

Chapter Fifteen
Dealing with It

Although she repeatedly insisted it was totally against normal practice, a harassed Matron Matteson eventually yielded to the pressure from Herbert Mabey to place his daughter in the Cottage Hospital's sole private room for the period of her recovery. The matron's only consolation, she comforted herself, would be in the size of the bill he would be asked to pay.

When informed that his daughter was sleeping and could not be visited, he had at first demanded that she be taken home to recuperate, but the matron had successfully argued against this. Mrs Stoker would need, for the next few days, the professional care available only in the hospital. After that, with further care and rest, she would become fully fit again.

It was a little after nine o'clock on the morning after the stillbirth. The patient's husband was a silent witness to this exchange in the matron's office, where an extra chair had been placed to allow all three to be seated.

"Even so," the matron continued sternly, making no attempt to hide her disapproval of both the discussion and of Herbert Mabey, "I am afraid she can receive no visitors until this afternoon. There will be far too much going on for the next few hours to permit any exceptions. Even for you, Mr Stoker." She turned to Charlie as she spoke the final few words, her tone softening dramatically.

"I am truly sorry," she whispered.

The solicitor rose huffily from his chair.

"Very well," he snapped. "Come, Charlie we'll go to the office."

Charlie made no attempt to follow. Instead, he said, "No, sir, you go on. I don't think I want to go to the office this morning. I must go to Hackney and tell my mother what has happened."

"Nonsense, dear boy! You can call her on the telephone from my office."

"Thank you, but no. I shall do it my way, Mr Mabey."

The solicitor stood for a moment, rather like a balloon that has been pricked and is slowly deflating. Then he said, "Hmmph!" and stalked out.

Charlie looked across to the now smiling matron.

"Matron, I don't think you have actually said. How is Margret? Does she know? How has she reacted?"

"No, Mr Stoker, she is still unaware of the situation. She has not properly awakened yet. She has been through an extremely traumatic experience—you both have, of course—but your wife has been deeply sedated, you understand. We have her under constant surveillance in a private room, and the nurse will advise me when she is in a condition to converse."

She glanced at the watch on her bosom.

"That could be at any time, now. Do you wish to be there to tell her yourself? I see that you are much more your normal self this morning. You appear to have handled that terrible shock remarkably well."

"Yes, well, I'm not sure about that. I am still reeling, really. But, knowing my wife, I think it may be better if it comes from me. You think it will be soon, do you?"

"Yes. Have a cup of coffee with me. I expect her to be awake by ten o'clock." She pressed a button on her desk and a there was an almost immediate tap on the door. She ordered two cups of coffee.

Charlie smiled at her. "The private room?" he asked, a twinkle in his eye.

Matron Matteson smiled broadly.

"It is standard procedure," she replied, "but I am used to dealing with the Herbert Mabeys of this world. He may be a big fish solicitor in Enfield, but he is the same size as anyone else in my hospital!"

The coffee was brought in and the matron excused herself for a couple of minutes. When she returned, she explained that if Margret were to ask the nurse attending her about the baby, she would be told she had given birth to a boy, and no more. The nurse would call for them at once. Quite soon afterwards, as they were finishing their coffee, a nurse popped her head round the door to say Mrs Stoker was awakening and asking for water. The matron said, "Thank you, nurse," and glanced at Charlie inquiringly.

He stood up at once.

"After you, then, Mr Stoker. The nurse will lead you to your wife. I shall be standing nearby in case you need me."

The nurse led Charlie down a corridor and into a small room facing out to the rear of the hospital. Margret was lying, half propped up on pillows, sipping a cloudy liquid. She was clearly not yet free of the effects of morphine, but she saw and recognised him at once. Her face brightened weakly as he leaned over her and kissed her gently.

"Hi, Margie," he said casually, grinning.

"My name is Margret!" she snapped, but with the sharpness of a very blunt knife. She said,

"Don't make me laugh, Big Boy!"

Her voice was weak and she paused, settled herself on the pillows. Then, looking around: "Where's our baby boy? I thought she'd gone to fetch him."

Charlie knew no easy way to say what was to follow, but his instincts told him the only way was the Stoker way. He took her hand and held it tight.

"He didn't make it, Marg. He was dead on delivery."

For a moment or two she stared at him, as if he were still kidding her. Then her body stiffened, her stare now reflecting the assimilation of his words. She began to shudder.

"No," she said, "no!" The second time with the rising tones of panic or fury. "No, it's not possible. He can't be dead! He was kicking and jumping. My baby can't be dead! No, No, No!!!"

She screamed the final 'no', threshing with her arms and trying to get out of bed. From nowhere, the matron appeared, shoving Charlie aside as she and the nurse restrained Margret.

She took her distraught patient's arm and inserted a needle. Margret gradually subsided, sobbing with vacant eyes into unconsciousness.

Matron Matteson grasped Charlie firmly by the arm and guided him swiftly back to the room adjoining her office. She pushed him into a chair. Charlie's face was colourless, his eyes wide.

He had not known exactly what to expect when Margret learned the facts but had never considered a situation he could not handle. Of course he had not adequately considered that he was dealing with Margret at her most distraught; and with her stomach having been ripped apart just twelve hours earlier.

He felt deeply ashamed. The matron placed a large brandy into his hand.

"Drink it," she commanded.

He obeyed. The spirit soon had its effect and Charlie regained some colour and some calm.

"Don't be too hard on yourself, Mr Stoker. That was just about par for the course, I'm afraid. There is no easy way to break that news to a woman who has felt life growing inside her for nine months. I have given her a dose to make her sleep for about four hours so that her body can settle down. Shall I send for a car to take you back to Clay Hill to get some rest?"

"No, matron. I shan't go to Clay Hill. I think I'll walk to the station, the air will do me good. I must go to see my mother. She lives in Amhurst Road, Hackney, and knows nothing of this yet."

"Very well, Sir. Come back at about 4 pm. and your wife should be anxious to see you. No one else will be allowed to visit her before you have returned."

She reached to open the door for him. He stood up and did something most unlike Charlie Stoker. He leaned over her and fleetingly kissed her forehead. He said,

"Thank you, Matron Matteson, you are a remarkable woman."

"Pshaw, Mr Stoker! I am merely a well-trained nurse. I suspect it is you who may be remarkable. I look forward to seeing you later today."

* * *

The shoe repair business at Amhurst Road was thriving despite the general economic gloom of the country. Billy Walters had visibly grown in stature with the maturity of marriage. By the spring of 1930, the pressure of work in the shop was dictating that a regular helper be found. The business could now afford one and Billy surprised Millie by suggesting that his wife, Sally, be considered.

Sally had kept her job at the Home and Colonial grocery store when she married, but the wages were very low and Billy was keen for her to work with him. Together, they would build the cobbling business so that they could afford a home of their own and start a family. Millie agreed at once. It was a splendid idea. Having the bright young pair in the basement would be good for the business, as well as company for her during the day.

Since the wedding, contact between Millie and Charlie had been no more than once a week, at best. The marriage arrangement, with the young couple living at Clay Hill, was not what either Stoker would have chosen. Millie, in particular, hated the emptiness of her home at night without Charlie. She pined for the daily sight of him and the sound of his heavy tread coming through the door, her handsome blond son with his father's build and twinkling eyes.

As ever, Father Peter was there to confide in and to receive spiritual comfort from, but the rest of the world saw only her self-possessed public face.

Stephen Collick was the exception. The diffident bachelor dropped in for a chat whenever he was passing, and they had visited the theatre and the ballet together, as well as taking day trips to the country. He had proved himself to be exactly what he had desired to be, a good friend.

He repeatedly told her how thrilled he had been to have the privilege of escorting the Stokers to the wedding. On that day he had been able to provide support for her through what would otherwise have been a difficult experience. And he continued to offer warm friendship and constancy.

As she made her way to the stairs on her way to the kitchen, at about midday on a Friday (the calendar in her bedroom/office had just reminded her it was the first day of August), her self-possession was shattered by the sight of the front door opening and Charlie entering the house. However great her delight at his unexpected arrival, her bewilderment, when he grinned, placed his arms around her and hugged her, was even greater.

He released her and she stared up at him, seeing at once beyond the big smile to the dark rims around the eyes and the grey colour of his cheeks.

"Oh, Lord protect us! What is wrong, Charlie?"

Charlie grasped his mother's hand and led her into the sitting room. Quite suddenly, he felt weak at the knees. He pushed her onto the sofa and dropped down heavily beside her.

"It's Margret, she's lost the baby. It was still-born."

"Oh, God, No!"

Millie, with a sharp intake of breath, remained utterly still, hand to her mouth. Charlie's eyes were full. He forced himself to breathe slowly and deeply. His mother placed her hand upon his arm, but uttered no word until she was sure he had calmed himself and regained control. Then she said:

"Be strong, Charlie, my love. It is the will of God. The Lord chooses to test our family to the utmost limit, and this is yet another trial. You are a Stoker and have been blessed with the strength of your blood, but it is not for us to know the ways of the Lord. We can only pray and accept."

Charlie did not reply. He lacked his mother's religious conviction but understood its importance to her. Her words about God's ways carried little weight with him, but she had said two words that carried comfort deep into his heart; possibly, he thought, for the first time in his life.

His mother had said 'my love'. Charlie had no memory of her ever having used such a term of endearment other than to his father. He turned and drew her to him in a close embrace. For the first time since before *that* day, he felt truly loved by his parent. He whispered, "I love you, Mum," as they clung to each other through their tears.

* * *

Charlie arrived back at the little hospital at the promised time in the afternoon. Matron Matteson was about to go off duty, but she took the time to explain that his wife was now awake and able to receive him. She also confided that she had instructed the Mabey family not to visit until 7.00 pm.

Charlie smiled his thanks and made his way to Margret's room. He found her, again propped up with pillows, looking pale and dark-eyed. She was staring intensely out of the window. She turned at his entrance and her face lightened for a moment, almost smiling, before darkening again.

"Hi, Margie," he greeted her with a smile, leaning down to kiss her. She moved her head to one side to present him with a cheek. He dutifully kissed it and stood up with a shrug.

"How're you doing, old girl? You've had a tough time, but you'll be okay now. Big Boy's here."

"Don't be flippant, Charlie, I'm not in the mood."

Charlie sat down on the wooden bedside chair and lit a cigarette. It was cloudy outside, a humid welcome to August, and the atmosphere in the hospital was just as heavy. He blew a few smoke rings and studied the plain walls of the little room, almost filled by the bed, the bedside cabinet and the chair. A wash basin stood in the corner.

Margret had resumed her intense glare at the window.

"Margret," he said, slightly stressing her name to emphasise the rejection of flippancy, "I know it's all gone wrong, but we are still here and we have to move on. If I could have suffered your torment and pain for you, I would willingly have done so."

He shrugged.

"I suppose you know that, but it doesn't lessen the pain, does it?"

He flicked ash into a small rubbish bin and passed his hand through his hair as he drew again on the cigarette. Margret turned and stared at him, her eyes cold and fierce.

"Go away, Charlie," she said flatly.

Charlie remained where he was, silent and smoking. After a long pause, Margret spoke again.

"The whole year has been one great waste of time," she said, softly at first, as much to herself as to her husband; but then, with rising bitterness: "a year of pain, of accommodation, of nine months sweat and a dead foetus, and all for what? To kill the only chance of salvation, of justification. And all this because of a mistimed coitus!"

Charlie blinked, and crushed the cigarette under his foot. "Whoops!" he said.

He sat for some time before giving up all hope of further progress at that visit. Having exploded, Margret had relapsed into the silent staring with which she had greeted him. He smoked three cigarettes before kissing her cheek and promising to see her the next day.

On the walk back to Clay Hill, he met his mother-in-law travelling in the opposite direction. Mairead had spoken by telephone with Matron Matteson just after Charlie had arrived at the hospital. On discovering that Mr Mabey would not be with her, the good matron had relented about the visiting times and suggested she call any time after 5.00 pm.

Charlie warned Mairead that Margret was in a bad humour, but suggested that after a day's rest she would be far more reasonable. Mrs Mabey gave a short laugh, as if she doubted it.

She was pleased, she said, that he looked more like his usual self now, but no doubt he could do with a good rest. A cold buffet had been laid out in the dining room for him and for whomever else was at home. Herbert had been called away by an important client and would not return until late. She had no idea what Harry's plans were, but he rarely came home except to sleep, and Terence had gone to stay with a friend in the country.

The house was indeed unoccupied, except for Jane, the maid who relieved Betsie for her rest days. She was also called upon whenever Mairead Mabey felt extra help was needed. Charlie ate a supper of cold meats, scotch eggs, tomato salad and potatoes, with home baked bread and butter and a bottle of ale. As soon as he finished eating, he realised how very tired he was. He made his way to the little suite he regarded as a stopping place rather than a home.

He thought again about Margret's outburst. He could well understand the thrust of it—the loss of their baby completely wrecked the point of every decision they had made. And if he were honest with himself, she was probably right. The fateful coupling had just been 'a romp'. Their marriage was, whether or not loveless, at best a marriage of obligation; of moral duty for him and for his mother; and one of convenience for Herbert Mabey.

At the hospital he had felt guilty as he sat by her bed, watching her anger and her pain. It was alright for him, wasn't it? The truth of it was, they had lost a baby they should never have been having—she should never have been having. And what had he done beyond enjoy a romp and live an interesting year?

He knew the answer to that, and it burned him. He had married her. He had married her knowing that there was no love between them. He had married her knowing that Margret would never be like her mother or his mother. He had married her knowing that Margret was not born to be a wife. He had married her so that he could be a father to his child, and care for it and watch it grow, so that he could be the father he himself had so missed.

And Margret's stare had said one thing more, hadn't it? It had said the game is over.

* * *

Before Charlie's wedding, Millie had had a lean-to extension built onto the back of the house, enabling her to separate the kitchen from the dining room. It meant sacrificing a little of her garden space but was well worth the compromise. The result gave her genuine dining space in the house, making entertaining guests at home a far more comfortable affair, not that she had many visitors.

This weekend, though, she would have two gentlemen for lunch. An invitation to Stephen had been made more than a week earlier, but then, to her delight, Charlie suggested that he would come back to Hackney after he had visited Margret on Saturday. He would stay the night in his old room and return to see his wife again on Sunday afternoon.

Charlie had made the suggestion to his mother on Friday simply seeing it as an opportunity to spend some time with her. After his visit to Margret and a night at Clay Hill, however, he realised he had to get away from there to work things out. His whole life situation would have to be reconsidered very carefully. Margret's words had indicated chillingly that, for her, the game was over. Yes, the game was over for him too, but their lives were not. Somehow, he told himself, they had to rebuild their marriage. They would have to rebuild it on solid ground, not on the sand of an unwanted pregnancy.

His return to the hospital on Saturday cemented the conviction in his own mind, but it was obviously not the time to discuss it. He found Margret much improved physically. She now had a little colour in her never rosy cheeks, and she was sitting in the bed at a more comfortable angle, able to move her body a little.

Emotionally, though, she was frigid. He received a cold cheek to kiss and a colder stare to smile at. He received perfunctory responses to his attempts at conversation. He smoked a few cigarettes in silence, trying to think of a way to break through the irrational barrier between them, before concluding that it did not matter. Margret was a highly intelligent and extremely practical person. When the physical wound had healed sufficiently, her head would clear and she would see things from a different perspective. Of that, he was confident. He left for Hackney at about 3.00 pm.

In reply to Millie's enquiry about Margret when he reached Amhurst Road, he said only, "She's still in shock, but progressing slowly." Over a cup of tea and a large piece of Madeira cake, however, he detailed fully the story of his visits to his wife. He told his mother the conclusions he had come to in the last twenty-four hours. Millie, superb confidante that she was, listened intently until he had told all. Then she said,

"More tea. Drink, you need the goodness."

Charlie laughed despite himself.

"So that's what you think, is it? Drink another cup of tea and it will all go away?"

"No, not quite, Charlie, but it can only help."

She refilled his cup. "How quickly is Margret expected to recover? She is a strong girl, not too long, I should think, but months rather than weeks?"

"Hmm, yeah, probably a couple of months. That's what her mother said this morning."

"I rather agree. So, as you seem to be sure about what you want to do, why don't we talk it over with Stephen tomorrow? It is the sort of thing he will know about."

For two people so unused to showing their true feelings, that Saturday evening was one to remember. It was as if, when Charlie had hugged his mother so tightly the previous day, when he had whispered those words, they had cut through the veil that had so long inhibited their relationship. For the first time in years, neither felt the need to withhold or disguise their thoughts, to be on their guard. They ate supper; they washed up the dishes together; they played cribbage at the dining table, listening to a concert of light music on the wireless; and they chatted about anything and everything.

It was, at last, the sort of relationship Millie had enjoyed with her husband Charles before 1917, but never totally after his return. It was the relationship with her son that she had yearned for. It was a loving relationship.

As for Charlie, he had been a sunny child. He had been warm and open and chatty—except, perhaps, with his stern mother—until *that* day had changed the world. He would never forget the chill stillness that had exuded from the basement and had enveloped him on *that* day; nor the feeling that his mother's rejection in her own moment of despair, had locked him inside that chill cloud. Now, four years later, he had been released: the world could be enjoyed in full colour again.

Chapter Sixteen
Autumn 1930 – A New Start

Charlie had come to three major decisions at the end of that tumultuous couple of days at the beginning of August. However, it was not until several weeks later that he was able to discuss them calmly with Margret.

Her anger had subsided, eventually, to be followed by a tearful period lasting about a week. Thereafter, she had slept a great deal, but she also began to make a conscious effort to be reasonable to visitors: her husband, her parents, and Jennifer, who also visited on several occasions. The conversations were always light, mostly trivial, but they had the desired effect. After three weeks, Dr Leghorn pronounced her well enough to convalesce at home, and she was released from Matron Matteson's care.

Only after she had been back at Clay Hill and had rested there for some days, did she indicate, in the privacy of their rooms, that she was ready to discuss their situation seriously. She had come to realise that motherhood was not something she was prepared to endure. There would be no more romping and no more mistakes. There would be no more pregnancies.

Then, in a perfectly reasonable tone, she told Charlie that she wanted to end the marriage. She intended to return to college and to become an academic.

The speech was met, as so often, by silence. Charlie opened his cigarette case and withdrew two cigarettes. He lit them both and passed one to Margret. She thanked him with a sardonic smile, gazed at him for a moment, then said:

"You are a decent man, Charlie Stoker. I feel for you more than I could ever feel for any other man, you know that. But I am not a decent woman. I can never be a decent wife. I shall never be any sort of wife. We must call it a day and get the marriage annulled."

Charlie laughed, "You know better than that, Margie." He shrugged.

"But, okay, let's sort things out. As far as you are concerned it has all been a game and now the game is over and you want your ball back. Right?"

She executed an exaggerated shrug but did not respond. Charlie drew on his cigarette.

"Well it doesn't work like that, Margret. We both played your game. We both enjoyed the game and we both said 'I do' in a church. That was not a casual decision, it was not part of your game. But it is a part of our life."

He paused to inhale again while watching for reaction. Margret just looked at him, waiting. Charlie exhaled a huge cloud of smoke.

"So, what can we do? Well, I've thought about it a lot and I think I know what to do. The first thing we must do is to get out of here. The atmosphere in this house is cold, it's sinister. You have always found it so, and now so do I. Your brothers both parade their hostility and your parents live in their own dark world. So, we move out at once."

"The second thing is, you resume your studies and I get myself another job. I must work, but I have to leave the legal profession.

"The third thing is how we live. We get along well, you and I, in good air. I don't give a damn about the romping, and if you want us to live separately within our home, that's alright with me. If you want to live together as man and wife, that's also alright with me. But we are married, and we shall live under one roof. Our private arrangements will be exactly that, private between us. And they must remain so."

Margret stared out of the window for a long time. Then she turned to her husband with a look of admiration.

"You've done it again, haven't you, Big Boy? You are a real man. When it comes to the big decisions you are as solid as a rock! But where would we move to, and what job would you get?"

Charlie's eyes twinkled. "The Collick Estate is having up to eight houses built on land they own to the east of the estate, near Chigwell. Some are near completion and Stephen Collick has said one of them is mine if I want it. I understand they are to be substantial detached dwellings, individually designed, each with three, four or five bedrooms, and standing on plots of about a quarter of an acre."

"That sounds pretty impressive. Have you not seen them?"

"No. I wanted us to have this conversation first. The house is no good to me if you don't agree."

"Don't agree? You idiot! Of course I agree! It is a perfect solution. You really are the most decent man, Charlie. I do not deserve this. Can we go to see them?"

She paused, and her eyes flickered for a moment. Then a new thought struck her.

"But how is it all to be financed?"

"Yes, well, in the circumstances, Margie, it will be important that we jointly own the property. Before we married, your father promised a settlement of five hundred pounds when the time came to move to our own house. I suggest we use that to pay half the price, and I shall cover the other half."

"That settlement money is half yours, Charlie. I have my own money. I shall provide another two hundred and fifty. What is the actual price?"

"I don't know yet. I understand the Estate expects to realise between one and two thousand pounds as an average. They are each to be finished to the purchaser's design, so the actual costs vary. Stephen said that three are already spoken for, but any of the others is ours and our total bill will be less than one thousand pounds, whatever we choose."

"Good gracious! That is astonishing. But how will you find the balance? You don't have the resources and you won't have a job!"

"Yes, I shall. I am going to work for Stephen Collick. He will provide the balance as a private loan that I shall repay from income."

"Well, I'll be blessed! Charlie Stoker, we must go to Chigwell as soon as possible. I shall be allowed to travel out in two weeks' time, we can go then. What sort of job will you do for Lord Collick?"

"Not Lord Collick, I said Stephen Collick—I've never met Lord Collick! I really don't know what it's about yet. Collick business interests range from textiles to newspapers to houses. Stephen talked about learning the business, but I don't know what business. My father worked in their print works, it could well be there. I shall find out soon. In the meantime, we must tell your parents at once about the house and the planned move, but we should not, for the moment, tell your father of my intention to leave Cavendish, Brigham, Mabey."

* * *

The loyal Jennifer had continued to visit Margret each Wednesday afternoon throughout the summer. Quite often, she stayed to have a meal with them in the evening, but after the loss of the baby she invariably left earlier, so as not to tax her sick friend. Margret's physical condition, however, began to show rapid improvement as her mind concentrated less on the pain of the tragedy and more on the promise of a new home and a bright future. There was further comfort for her in the announcement of her excellent examination results from the LSE. She felt spurred to regain her strength and to get back to her studies.

The examination results from the Northern had also been published, and all four friends had done well. Jennifer had passed her intermediate examination and was looking forward to her final year and a B Pharm degree. Daphne had also passed, achieving the intermediate qualification of Ph.C. She had already returned to work at the Lacey Pharmacy, where, as a qualified pharmacist, she could be left in charge of the dispensary and command a higher wage.

For Bobby, now twenty-one years old, the award of the coveted diploma in mechanical engineering was the culmination of six years' hard work as apprentice and student. He was now free to set up his own motor-cycle repair shop, his and his father's dream. This meant the end of his Saturday mornings with Charlie, but, as two working men, they made a new arrangement to swim together on Thursday evenings. It also meant that he and Daphne were in a much stronger position to plan and to save for their wedding the following summer.

Charlie had sailed through his second-year exams. Whatever direction his life was about to take, he was determined to complete his studies. He had met with the principal, and had been granted permission to complete his final year at evening classes. When the principal had remarked that he was taking on a great deal, Charlie had replied, twinkle-eyed, that if his father could do it at the old Finsbury Tech. in 1905, it would be a piece of cake for him at the Northern in 1930.

Charlie had no idea what work Stephen Collick had in mind for him, whether it would be in the print works or elsewhere; but whatever it should be, it would be a more satisfying challenge than the solicitor's office in Enfield. For the moment, however, he would continue conscientiously enough where he was, at least until it was time to inform his father-in-law of his intentions; but he detested the place, with its miserable, nervy atmosphere and its currents of antagonism.

Margret had retained her room at the university and stayed there for two or three days each week during the new term, leaving Charlie to stay at Clay Hill without her for those nights. He was quite stoic about it, now accustomed to the dark atmosphere of the Mabey household.

They had explained to Margret's parents their need to break away and to set up their own home, and this had been accepted not too reluctantly by the Mabeys. Herbert Mabey had agreed to honour his offer of five hundred pounds, the decision greatly influenced by the opportunity to do business with the Collicks. The link encouraged his hope of establishing a lucrative relationship with the Estate.

The four-bedroomed house at Chigwell was not completed until the end of the year. It was an extravagantly spacious home for the young couple and was furnished in an attractive, somewhat spare, art-deco style. The immediate impression throughout was of light. From a wide hallway, with magnolia walls and oak parquet flooring, a staircase led up, via a landing, where a large window looked out to the rear of the house, to the four bedrooms and the marble finished bathroom.

One reception room and two of the four bedrooms had been left completely unfurnished for the time being. They explained to visitors that they wanted to take their time and not rush to furnish them in a manner they may later regret. In fact, the new Stoker home was designed so that it could, if necessary, be divided into two self-contained residences. It occupied the end plot of the designated building land, adjoining farmland also owned by the estate; and, alongside, there was a two-acre paddock for Margret's horse, an extra present from Stephen.

When everything was signed and sealed for the impending move from Enfield to Chigwell, Charlie informed Herbert Mabey of his career decision. He thanked his father-in-law for the opportunity he had made possible, and for the several months of invaluable experience gained. Reluctantly, though, he had decided that his talents were not suited to a legal career. He would revert to his original plan of completing his physics course at evening classes while earning a wage in one of the Collick factories.

Mabey accepted the inevitable disappointment with little grace.

Mr and Mrs Stoker moved into their new home two months after Charlie's twentieth and just in time for Margret's twenty-first birthday, in January 1931. Since the loss of the baby, Margret had reverted very much to the character Charlie recognised from the early days of their association: independent, aloof, fiercely guarding her personal space.

The essential difference now, though, was that her tirades were reserved for others. She treated Charlie with respect. They trusted each other as friends.

They were friends, though, who did not romp. Romping was a thing of the past. In the new house, they occupied separate bedrooms.